Cygne
Rouge

F. V. Pires

ISBN: 978-0-9966019-0-0

The author dedicates this story to all you hard-hatted women who yearn for romance. Put on your tango shoes. If you can walk, you can dance.

.

CONTENTS

ACKNOWLEDGMENTS

Without the help of friends and family, this book would not be possible. Thank you to all who helped. You know who you are.

CHAPTER 1

I pondered at some length the colorful display on the monitor. As always, it looked like it ought to be right. That's always the first impression. It's not until you get there and start testing that you can see all the inconsistencies and sometimes downright dangerous mistakes. But I wasn't there yet, and from the remote vantage point of my cozy office, it all looked fine. Just as my life might look when viewed from the right distance.

"Miranda, I need to talk to you." Lu, the new hire—the perfectly thin, fashionably attired, ravishing new hire—entered my office. She looked at me seriously, fingering her gold necklace, arms folded.

"What's up, Lu?" I asked. She walked over to my desk and stared at the animated display. Then she turned and quickly, silently, closed the office door.

"I am very worried about the assignment Dan has given me."

"The Carolina project? What's the problem?" We all knew Lu was to go on site with two of the senior

1

personnel. It looked like it might be a long project and everybody was half-expecting to be sent at some point for a three- to four-week stint.

"I'm just not familiar with the process. I've asked several times for some reference materials and all I get is 'don't worry about it.' But I am worried. Then finally Dan gave me a pile of charts and diagrams, but they don't seem to be for this plant. They're for some other plant. He said that's the closest thing they have to reference materials. I don't see how I'll be of any use." Poor Lu. Straight out of college, where problems are well defined and the answer is in the back of the book.

"Well, you'll just have to learn the plant from the inside out, like the rest of us," I replied sympathetically. "The real world doesn't always have a manual, ya know?"

"I am supposed to work with Ben and Schaeffer for two weeks straight. Ben hates me. I really think he hates me, Miranda. He will watch me all the time to catch any mistakes before I can fix them. I know he didn't want to hire me! He's going to give a bad report no matter what I do. Please, give me some advice." Ah, the truth of the matter.

"Do a great job and impress him." I've always been really bad at advice. Ljudmila Dineva rolled her fetching brown eyes and looked at me like the simpleton I surely am. Everyone knew that Ben didn't want to hire her. But we expected his essential fairness to prevail. Schaeffer was clearly sweet on Lu, had defended her since he set eyes on her at the job interview, and would surely finesse any issues that might arise in the next few weeks. I wasn't particularly worried.

The girl was a bit of an enigma. She had a first-class degree from Georgia Tech, and all the references you could want. But she gave such an impression of helplessness, liberally sauced with panic, that it made a person wonder if all the praise was real. Layered over all of it was a thick, almost defensive, femininity.

Lu threw her cashmere sweater over her shoulders and walked gracefully out of my office in the highest pair of heels ever seen inside our building. A faint air of perfume followed her. I had to concur with my coworkers' universal appraisal of her. Both those in favor and those opposed to her hire agreed: This is one unusual engineer.

Tammy and I slid between the rows of hanging clothes, so tightly packed that I had to grab three hangers at a time just to be able to get the clothes off the rack. I held up a sheer navy blouse that looked like it could possibly be silk, although at that price it clearly wasn't.

"What will you wear it with?" Tammy eyed the blouse suspiciously.

"Jeans," I said, "on a date." I knew the next question would be "Where?"

Tammy groaned. Today we had a deal. No single purchases, only complete outfits were to be purchased. If you couldn't find the whole outfit in the store, it was a no-go.

"Jeans," Tammy explained, "are the last refuge of the scoundrel. Anything goes with jeans. Jeans are not part of an 'outfit.' No buying jeans today! Think of something else."

I thought about the possibility of a date. It helped to think about a particular date, namely the one I was going to have on Friday with Andy. We would take a walk in the park, have dinner somewhere nice, and then go listen to some music. Andy loved the Irish sessions at the bar in midtown, especially when the bagpiper showed up. I liked them too, but I was hankering after something edgier. I was hoping to talk Andy into the Latin jazz at the Pinktown Diner—worse beer but better martinis. I had little hope of success.

I stared at the navy blouse. Maybe a skirt? I had a lot of skirts already. Why is it that when I buy a new blouse it never matches any skirt I already own?

"Does that blouse match any of the skirts you already own?" Tammy looked me in the eye and knew the answer. She took the navy blouse away. "Let's see if we can find one that looks good with it," she said, and led me around the store, flying the blouse like a flag in front of us. Tammy found three potential skirts and I found a pair of non-jeans and a camisole to wear under the sheer blouse. Tammy browsed the racks for herself, choosing a hot pink blouse with white flecks, a tight khaki skirt, and a pair of floral shorts of modest length. She also found several sweaters and two scarves. Tammy has more scarves than seems normal. We retired to the dressing rooms to try it all out.

I put on the camisole and blouse, then added the lower pieces. All of the skirts fit but the non-jeans were hopeless. I came out of the stall in the first outfit and looked in the mirror. Tammy had picked a short plaid skirt with a bit of navy in it. It was a traditional pattern but a very modern cut, and would look great with black tights and some nice shoes. I imagined that Andy could look at the plaid skirt whenever he missed the Irish session. It would remind him of the bagpiper, who for some reason insisted on wearing a plaid Scots kilt while playing Irish pipes.

"Hey, that's not bad at all!" Tammy appraised my outfit. She was wearing the hot pink blouse with the khaki skirt, topped with a beige sweater that had a thin orange stripe down the arms. All of this was finished with a scarf that looked like Picasso had collaborated with Harold and his Purple Crayon. It was stylish without being ridiculous. Tammy was good at this. She could always figure out where the line ought to be and find a way to put one toe over it. I was pleased that she liked my outfit. "Try on the next skirt!" she demanded.

My next skirt was a cheap stretchy thing covered in sequins and very short. Tammy pondered it.

"So, what do you want from Andy?" She finally said. "Do you want to keep it at dinner and music? Do you want him to fall for you? Do you want to slam him in the stomach with an outfit like this?"

I honestly had no answer. I had been seeing Andy for months. It was pleasant. It was fun. It was friendly, warm, and, well, comfortable. Comfortable is a really nice thing. I catalogued his virtues in my mind and had an urge to forget about the Latin jazz club and buy an air ticket to Brazil. Not Rio either, but some jungle-filled corner of Brazil with mosquitoes and large reptiles. I guess comfort is not my thing. Did I want to slam him in the stomach with a sexy outfit? I had no idea. I went back into the dressing room and tried on the third skirt.

When I came out, Tammy was studying her second outfit in the mirror. This time it was a shiny leopard print dress. I felt that Tammy had lost sight of the line or intentionally jumped over it. She smiled at herself in the mirror and added a wide belt to the ensemble. Suddenly the dress had a retro feel. She layered a short black sweater and the whole thing almost looked reasonable, if teetering on the edge of vintage. She pulled her hair up into a bun. I sighed.

"And where will you ever wear that?" I didn't really expect an answer.

"To Steve's company Christmas party," she replied without hesitation. "Every guy wants the other guys to think he has the trophy girlfriend. It's the least I can do. I'll wear the longest, most sparkling earrings I have. And what have we here?" She turned her attention to me.

My third skirt was a flouncy item that had a nice swirl to it, in a metallic print that complemented the more conservative blouse. Tammy handed me her wide black belt and I put it on.

"Where are you going with Andy on Friday?" For Tammy, clothes were never really about clothes. I explained the Irish/Latin quandary. "And exactly how bored are you with the Irish music?" was her next question.

"I can hum all the tunes," I replied.

In the end I bought two of the three skirts. They were cheap enough and they all looked good on me. We hit all the shoe stores, circling like sharks, and I found some heels that looked good with both of the skirts. We laughed and joked and had some light dinner. Over a shared dessert Tammy asked me which of the two skirts I was planning to wear on Friday. I was indecisive. She took the bag from me, and handed it back with only the flouncy skirt in it.

"I'm keeping the plaid one until after Friday, so you will wear this one," she said, adding, "dress for the date you want, not the date you have."

"I thought you were going to Kannapolis with Schaeffer and Lu." I met Ben at the coffee pot a few days later.

"I asked Dan to send someone else." Ben avoided my eyes.

"Who?" Our firm is usually blessedly free from intrigue, so Ben's lack of explanation stood out as an evasive maneuver. I wouldn't let it stand.

"Tanner," Ben said quietly, scurrying away to avoid further questions. I followed him to his office.

"What's going on? I thought Tanner was going to Port Charlotte with me next week." I wasn't upset. I can handle the Port Charlotte job by myself and I was looking forward to the Florida weather. Fall was over in the Boston area and the days had shortened noticeably. But I would miss Tanner, my best friend except for Tammy. We had been together at this job for quite a few years. Hanging out after work and joking about bosses and clients made both of our lives more bearable.

Ben gave up trying to avoid me and faced me squarely.

"She is driving me nuts. When she found out I was coming on the trip she didn't even say hello for two days. Then she came into my office and didn't leave for an hour. Then Schaeffer came into my office and gave me hell for another hour, just in case I hadn't had enough. They assume they know what I am thinking and then they get mad at me for it. I didn't say anything! And then, just when I thought I knew where I stood with both of them, she came back for another hour and tried to make nice. I can't take two weeks of it. Dan put me on one of the local projects."

With this explanation we parted, and I spent the day staring at the computer and wondering how any conversation with Lu could have upset Ben that much. At lunch there was email from Tanner:

Mimi love,

Here I am enjoying this task tremendously. The factory we converted to an ethanol plant last year we are now re-converting to its former self. Perhaps next year they will want it to be an ethanol plant again. Our employment is secure! And the entertainment is spectacular. Romance blooms. Can't wait to share.

Driving home after work I could barely restrain myself from calling Tanner, but I waited until I got home. I got him on the phone while I was getting ready to go out. Tanner was quite eager to fill me in on the first day at the plant.

"Mimi, you would never believe the amount of flirting that can go on between two people in hard hats and steel-toed shoes. Really, I might try to catch some of it on my camera tomorrow."

"Lu was in steel-toed boots?" Of course, I knew she would have to wear these on the job site. I just hadn't really imagined it until then. Tanner howled.

"Steel toed boots, a hard hat, mascara, lipstick, fire retardant overalls, and a matching silk scarf." At this, Tanner burst into song. He had the habit of suddenly singing when overcome with the possibilities of a situation. I loved to hang out with him, but this habit made him a lousy wingman. If I flirted with anyone while we were together I was likely to hear Tanner singing "I feel the earth move under my feet . . ." in the background, slowly rising in volume. Tanner was now belting out a vampy rendition of "Barbie Girl" with a fake Bulgarian accent. I sang along with him for a moment or two, then excused myself. Under other conditions I would have made a serious objection to the whole Barbie reference. But it was, after all, Tanner: the only gay guy in a company full of engineering jocks. He made me laugh whenever we were together, and I was prepared to overlook his tasteless moments, most of the time.

Pondering the likely impact of these developments on my work life, I was slow to get ready for the evening's activities. When Andy arrived at my door I was still fussing with my hair and makeup. Several silver necklaces, some earrings, and a black blazer enhanced the navy shirt and flouncy skirt. The new shoes clicked on the floor. Andy, dressed in his usual plaid shirt, sweater, and jeans, raised his eyebrows appreciatively. Together we entered the evening.

Sunday morning Tammy came over for brunch. We guzzled coffee and nibbled crispy bites of linguiça, the sausage of my childhood, with fresh French bread.

"I'm off to Port Charlotte tomorrow. I should be there about two weeks."

"That is too bad, because there's a play in Boston I thought you might want to see with me."

"Take Steve," I suggested. Tammy looked thoughtful.

"No," she said. "Somehow I don't think the Vagina Monologues are great date material. But I thought you might be interested, as the only girl in your firm."

"Not anymore," I reminded her. "Now I have Lu.

Except Lu is in Kannapolis making eyes at Schaeffer. I get daily reports from Tanner and believe me, it gets better every day." I pulled out my cell phone and showed her the latest sneaky photo Tanner sent. Schaeffer and Lu were looking up at some pipes in the ceiling of the factory. He was pointing something out, with his arm around her shoulder, holding her close. I could almost hear Tanner singing.

"Togetherness through engineering," Tammy studied the photo. "Is that fur?"

I looked more closely. Under the overalls and work shirt, sticking out at the collar, were bits of bluish fur. I texted Tanner immediately. Tammy and I read his prompt answer:

"I wondered if you would notice. A little item Schaeffer bought her. She wears it constantly."

Tammy and I wondered together. Ljudmila Dineva, I explained, was a young woman strong enough to leave her native country and obtain an advanced degree in engineering in a language that is neither her first, second, nor third. She found a job near Boston, negotiating whatever visa requirements stood in her way. She negotiated passage for at least one older relative, a grandmother perhaps, with whom she lives. She has, in her few years, surmounted more obstacles than most people will ever face. And yet there she is in the photo, wearing blue fur under her work shirt and overalls, taking instruction from Schaeffer, and looking helpless.

"She looks so lost," commented Tammy.

"I guess helpless is a relative state." I offered this explanation, even though I suspected that Lu's survival skills far outstripped anything Schaeffer could summon.

"A little helplessness is good for a relationship," observed Tammy. "It makes the other person feel needed. Even if it's fake."

"Latin jazz is very good for a relationship." I was teasing her because I knew she wanted to ask about Andy. She smiled and waited. "And the Pinkhouse Diner makes an awesome martini," I added.

"Did you wear the new outfit?" Tammy has a strong sense of cause and effect. "If you had bought that sequined skirt and worn it instead, he'd still be here this morning. Where did he take you for dinner?"

I gave her all the details, up to the point where we left the Pinkhouse Diner. Tammy was impressed. Over the last few months she had listened while I described our dates, which, while becoming steady and reliable had also become routine and predictable. It's funny how close "steady" is to "routine," and how close "reliable" is to "predictable." This last date was still with reliable Andy, but it was a little less predictable than usual. We stayed at the Pinkhouse Diner until the band quit. After, we went to a famous bar at the top of a hotel, with a romantic view of the city lights. That was Friday. Andy didn't stay until Sunday; that was true. But he did stay until Saturday.

"Just one more question." Tammy grinned at me. I wondered what she wanted to know. Surely she didn't have to ask if we made love.

"Did you catch the end of the bagpiper's set on the way home?"

CHAPTER 2

Port Charlotte is a sleepy little town full of seafood joints and retired people, enlivened by the occasional backyard alligator wandering out of the canals that crisscross the town. I had been there every year for the past four, always in November. I stayed at the hotel near the freeway, spent my days at the citrus processing plant nearby, and my evenings at the various local dives along the river and beaches. Usually Tanner was with me, but this time I was alone.

I drove down to one of the places at the mouth of the river with a deck out over the water. I intended to take complete advantage of the balmy weather before returning to the onset of the Boston winter. I ordered crab claws and a beer, pulled a book out of my purse and settled into a relaxing evening. Quiet country rock serenaded me from the direction of the bar, with its familiar yearnings for faithful lovers and big trucks. The sun set over the wide mouth of the river and the gulf beyond as little speedboats hurried home to dock.

At the next table a lively conversation was developing. I put the book away in favor of enjoying the bucolic ambience of the waning day and the excellent eavesdropping that is the primary entertainment of a public bar. The group at the next table was an unusual mix of ages. Several older couples mingled with a young couple, two middle-aged women and one thirty-something man who seemed to dominate the conversation without saying much at all.

"You are wasting your time at the mall," one of the older women declared. "Get the real thing. Use the Internet or drive to that store in Tampa."

"Things I buy over the Internet never fit," objected the young woman, "and they are so expensive."

"You can always send them back," offered her partner. I was sure they were together but I couldn't tell if they were married. I tried to scan for wedding rings without being noticed. The discussion continued hotly over the purchase of some item clearly of common interest but that I could not identify. Whenever someone offered an opinion, all eyes glanced at the quiet man, who replied by nodding, shaking his head, or raising his eyebrows with a smile.

Food arrived at their table but the conversation remained animated. One of the older women said something in French, and this made the quiet man quite excited.

"*Comme il faut!*" he exclaimed, "*Comme il faut* is what everybody wants. It might break your wallet but it won't improve upon what you have now, if what you now wear fits, fits securely, and is comfortable. Get them if you want, but you don't need them."

"I love these!" The older woman pulled from her purse a strappy high-heeled shoe. It looked like something Lu would wear to the office. I imagined Lu in her steel-toed boots, trying to look stylish, and the thought made me smile.

The man at the next table caught my eye and smiled back. He made a point of looking at my shoes. I was wearing some medium heels with my jeans, with the markings of a spectator pump and a secure t-strap around the ankle. Nothing too special, but they did take my usual jeans up a step. The man stood up and came over to my table.

"Excuse me, but would you mind showing my friends your shoes?" He offered me his hand graciously and led me to his table. I pulled my jeans up slightly to display my pumps.

"Notice," he said, taking my hand theatrically and guiding me in a circle around him, "that she walks securely. Her feet do not slide around in the shoes and the straps keep her ankle from wobbling." He took me in ballroom position, as if we were going to waltz.

"Please walk backwards with me for a few steps." He placed my weight on my left foot and slowly walked me backwards, step by step. My left hand pressed against his shoulder for guidance. He released the embrace and led me back to his friends.

"These would be perfect shoes for you," he said to the young woman. Immediately an argument arose.

"What are the soles made of?"

"Can she turn?"

"Do they stick?"

They all looked at me, the unexpected example of something I did not understand. I took off one shoe and gave it over to the group. Then, in a moment of surrender, I gave them the other shoe too. I went back to my table, got my beer, and returned to listen to the conversation. At their invitation, I moved my things, pulled up a chair, and became part of the party.

The quiet man, no longer quiet, held a shoe in each hand. At length he compared the features of my inexpensive pumps, with their man-made uppers and hard plastic soles, to the strappy spike-heeled beauties belonging to Cheryl, the older lady who had pulled them from her purse.

"The closed toe is protective, the sides come up in a supportive way, the straps are secure. The heel is high enough. In fact, you wouldn't want it any lower." He then turned both shoes over. The soles of my shoes were rubbery and gripped the floor pretty well. Cheryl's heels had soles of soft gray suede, so thin that it should have been made into gloves instead. On the instep was the inscription *Comme Il Faut.*

The man, whose name was Paolo, continued his analysis of the shoes. "These," he said, pointing to the spikes, "will turn brilliantly on a wood floor. If you were to wear them on the street they would be ruined. These others are made for the street and are meant to grip the floor. Not so good for dancing, but easy to fix."

The young woman, Colleen, wanted to know where to take a pair of shoes like mine to be resoled as slippery dance shoes. Paolo smiled.

"The hardware store," he explained. "Just cover the bottom with duct tape and you've got the perfect soles. Of course, you will have to recover them now and then, so buy a big roll." The whole group giggled, and Cheryl wondered aloud about the silver flashes of duct tape showing when dancers picked up their feet.

"Your feet are supposed to find the floor and stay near it!" admonished Paolo, adding, "You could always find black duct tape, which is sometimes called gaffer's tape."

"How about red?" I suggested. They looked at me and smiled. Paolo liked the idea, I could tell.

As the evening passed, I learned that this group of tango dancers, all students of Paolo's, met socially every Monday and took a lesson every Thursday. I was invited, indeed cajoled, to join them at their next practice. I was happy to say yes, because without Tanner to entertain me I looked forward to several weeks of solitary, boring evenings. When the group broke up, Cheryl and her husband, Don, escorted me to my car. There was something I wanted to ask Cheryl, and here was my chance.

"Why did you have those shoes in your purse?" Cheryl smiled at me and explained that she and Don were heading to a dance party in a nearby town. Even though it wasn't a tango event, she expected that some of the music would be suitable for the steps she and Don had been practicing for months.

"It pays to be prepared," was how she put it. I had to think of Tammy, insisting that I pack a dress and a skirt to take on a two-week job in a place where I knew nobody except the guys at the plant. Not that there was anything wrong with . . . most of them. But the nice ones were all thoroughly married.

"Yes," I agreed, "even if you don't know what you are preparing for!"

I arrived at the plant first thing Tuesday morning to find Carlos, the process engineer, swearing quietly in Spanish at the computer screen, which was black. You don't have to be a tech support genius to know that a black screen is not a good sign. He explained that this was the result of recent roof repairs, which left a hole in the roof over the computer for four days while he was away and the factory was down, during which a Florida deluge had swamped the room, all the electronic devices, and the computer that controlled the entire operation. The room smelled damp and musty, with a slightly stinky overtone. Nothing dries quickly in south Florida. Together we found the alternate computer, which fortunately was kept in a dry location, that held the backup I did the previous year. We installed it and got it up and running so I could start testing controls.

At lunch, Carlos grilled me about my life, and I returned the favor. I asked about his wife, his kids, his cousins, his parents, and his granny, all in self-defense. I didn't want to have to explain my own life.

"So," Carlos said, "are you still seeing that guy?"

"No," I admitted. I knew he was referring to Jim, the guy I was seeing last November. "Jim and I broke up. I'm seeing a new guy named Andy."

"So," Carlos continued, "you stopped going with Jim then you started going with Andy?"

"No," I admitted again. "There was a guy in between named Dave but he turned out to be gay."

"Tanner should have tipped you off." Carlos had always felt that Tanner was sent by the company, or perhaps by the cosmos, to protect me.

"Oh, he did," I explained, "as soon as he met him. And then he went out with the guy for a while. Later he told me I was lucky to get out of it so easy. I think Dave still calls him once a week."

Carlos chuckled. He looked forward to my visits and always welcomed me as if I were a visitor from some other, friendly, planet.

On the way back to work we swung by the nearest box store and I bought a hair dryer. I spent the rest of the day blow-drying the innards of the soggy computer. By the time I got it completely dry it was eight in the evening and I had just enough energy to pick up a sandwich and collapse in the hotel room.

I tried to read a few pages of the book I bought in the business section of the airport bookstore. It was one of the many thinly disguised self-help books repackaged for the business market. It catered to the neurotic fears of the visibly successful who were beginning to wonder if their life's work was of any real use. Drawing allegories between division managers and conductors of major symphony orchestras, it smoothly promoted an equivalence of cultural value that could never be argued rationally. I love these books. They make me smile and sometimes they make me laugh. Sometimes they even make a good point. I know the cultural value of my work. This week I'm going to make an orange juice factory function properly, thereby contributing to millions of breakfasts in America, where the presence of a glass of juice is taken completely for granted. I always hope one of these books will help me understand what I want from the part of my life that is not work, but they never do.

In the end I decided that it was time to check in with Tanner.

"Ciao, Mimi, I'm having the time of my life. A romantic comedy is unfolding before my very eyes. Every evening I am invited to dinner with two lovebirds that strain their self-control to the utmost until I excuse myself early. I look out my window and see them go off in the rental car after dinner, and I can hear their pleasant, inebriated voices when they return in the wee hours. I hear only one door open and shut. The next morning I round them up at breakfast and watch them crawl into the car, which I always offer to drive to the plant, where they are both useless until mid-afternoon. The chief engineer is beside himself and is ready to send them both home. I heard him talking on the phone with Dan yesterday. I think he is going to trade both of them for Ben."

"Sounds exciting," I admitted, glad I was as far from the situation as possible. I told Tanner about the tango dancers I'd met.

"Oh, I wish I were there!" he exclaimed. "I took some tango lessons a few years ago and always meant to get back to it. Make sure you have the right shoes."

"It's all about the connection! Keep your connection," Paolo chided the entire group of dancers, which was slowly revolving counterclockwise around him.

I walked backward, firmly connected to a gentleman twice my age and size, who stared resolutely over my head.

"Follow me, not the music," said my partner. To prove his point he took a series of steps, impossibly, improbably off the unmistakable beat of the slow tango that was playing. It was a strategy I didn't understand. Fortunately, Paolo instructed the men to move forward to the next woman in the circle, and I was dancing with Cheryl's husband, Don. He could see I was nervous.

"Just relax and lean toward me," he said reassuringly, "and try to follow my lead." Don walked slowly in time with the music, then he threw in some quicker steps two to a beat. "Very nice," he encouraged, "you have the basic step."

The basic step, as it turned out, was walking. But it was two people walking in perfect synchrony, which was harder than I ever imagined it could be. With Don securely guiding me, I let my mind wander a little. If walking together is so hard, imagine trying to live with someone else, or raise kids with him. I thought about Tammy and me, as yet unsuccessful in finding the right steady boyfriend. I thought about Carlos, with his job, spouse, kids, and extended family lined up in perfect harmony. Was it luck, or was there something there that could be learned and put to use? I resolved to ask him.

"Seek the floor with your heels," Paolo said for the third time that evening. I still wasn't sure what that meant. He came over to Don and me and stared at my feet while we moved, which was disconcerting. He waved Don away and took his place, walking me backward for a few steps.

"Don't lift your feet far off the floor. Keep them low, and when you step, get your heel onto the floor almost immediately. Tango dancers are not on their toes." I adjusted my step. Satisfied, he gave me back to Don and then moved the men forward once again.

By the end of the evening, we had tried out a few patterns in addition to the simplest step. But Paolo always returned regularly to the basic walk, emphasizing the connection with the partner, the feel of the low tango walk, and the rhythm of the music. I was starting to like the whole process. After class I went out for a beer with Cheryl and Don. When they learned where I was from and why I was in town, they immediately invited me to dinner on the weekend. I could begin to see the many ways that the tango class would be a boon to both my sanity and my social life for the next couple of weeks.

The input to a citrus processing plant is citrus. The output is juice and pulp, separated. The middle part is a bit more complicated. An arrangement of pumps, hoppers, centrifuges, more pumps, and holding tanks is controlled by a myriad of sensors for temperature, pressure, tank volume, and fluid flow. These sensors are all connected to a central computer, which displays a cartoon of the running factory, together with the numbers that describe the output of each sensor, and which may be used to control every aspect of the process. It is my job every November to make sure the cartoon is a correct representation of the factory, that the numbers on the screen correspond to the correct sensor in the plant, and that the controls used by the computer operator correspond to what they are supposed to on the factory floor.

Nature dictates when fruit ripens. In October it is safe to shut the factory down, as no fruit is harvested. Machines are taken apart, cleaned, and reassembled. A few weeks before the citrus season starts, I arrive and repair the controls. During the previous year some sensors or control units would have broken and been replaced—or not. Some won't look broken but they will not be functioning properly, giving an incorrect readout or doing the wrong thing when summoned. Sometimes broken things are repaired during the year by moving a working part from one area of the factory to another. This might cause the computer operator to believe that a pump has been turned off in one location when, in reality, it is in a completely different part of the plant. Throughout the year, as these improvisations are made, Carlos keeps the changes entirely in his head. Mostly. That is, they are in his head if they are anywhere.

The factory foreman stood next to me, hurling a string of obscenities in no particular direction. This year it seemed that an army of monkeys had been rearranging the factory control units and sensors. They also apparently rearranged many of the intermediate connections, so that the labels on junctions were complete fiction. It was going to be a big job.

"At least your main computer is going to be okay," I said, waving at the resuscitated machine in the middle of the room. The hair dryer lay at its side. "Do you keep a record of changes made during the year? That would speed this up considerably."

The foreman looked at me like I was a simple-minded idiot, which in some ways I am. I was not offended. We have this conversation every year. I already knew the answer to my question, which isn't really a question in the first place, but merely a suggestion for the next year—one that is never, ever followed.

Carlos took his half of the two-way radio and headed to the first set of hoppers and centrifuges. One by one he would turn on each device, prompt it to send a signal, and tell me where it was. I would stay in the musty control room and check where it appeared to be on the computer console, keeping a spreadsheet to track every device, its location, the reported location on the animated cartoon, and whether it gave any signal at all. I also checked last year's records and noted changes. It would take the better part of a week to complete this part of the work. Then I would have to correct the computer program.

At lunch I started my research project on Carlos.

"How is it that you and Anna get along so well together? I can't find anybody I want to be with every Friday, let alone all the time."

Carlos was thoughtful. I imagined him wondering how to explain the simplest facts of life to an alien from another planet.

"Well, Anna and I have been together so long we have sort of grown into each other," he finally replied. Then he thought the better of it and added, "We used to talk about how we would make sure that the other one got what they needed, did what they needed to do in life. But now it's more like we need the same things. So there's less of that discussion."

"I don't even know what my boyfriend really needs." Truly, I had never thought of Andy in those terms at all.

"Well," replied Carlos, "what do you need?"

I had to admit I didn't know. Carlos looked at me kindly. The poor space alien, if only she knew what she needed. Then perhaps she could go and find it.

That evening Dan called to hear an update on the citrus plant. I gave him my appraisal of the situation. It looked like I might be there for longer than planned. Before we got off the phone I put on my most innocent voice and asked how the Kannapolis project was going. There was a long, rather uncomfortable pause on the line.

"Mimi, I'm sure Tanner has kept you up to date on everything. So I think you must know that Ben is there now. Ljudmila and Schaeffer are back at the office. Schaeffer will be on his way to Ohio tomorrow. You know that project."

I was dying to ask what he was going to do with Lu. I hoped, for her sake, that he would give her a chance to do some work for one of my less besotted colleagues.

"Ljudmila," he said, reading my mind, "is here at the office, constructing a graphics program for the new plant in Syracuse."

"Sounds good." I liked the idea of keeping Lu under local supervision. I really hoped she would show her best work without the distraction of Schaeffer's constant attention. As I got off the phone with Dan, I saw that Tammy was trying to reach me. Looking forward to a long chat, I curled up in the armchair next to the window and returned the call. As soon as she picked up, I sensed something was wrong. Within moments of hearing my voice she began to cry.

"I don't even know what I want to say to him!" Tammy had gone to a movie with her cousin and seen Steve, the boyfriend for whom she had invested in a shiny leopard dress, out on an obvious date with some other girl. He had noticed Tammy, and she was getting frequent texts from him, asking to talk with her.

"You have to talk to him," I said, "because that is fair. You don't really know the circumstances."

Tammy sniffed.

"Did the two of you agree not to see other people?" I decided to take the most rational approach I could invent.

"Sort of." I could hear quiet sobbing, then "No, not really." Tammy was far too upset to have a reasonable conversation with Steve. I could see this. I made her agree to talk with him in the morning. She texted him, suggesting a time, then called me back again.

"But I still don't know what I could possibly say!" She burst into tears again. I thought about Carlos and Anna.

"Don't say anything," I suggested. "Just ask him what he needs."

Tammy stopped crying for a moment and thought this over.

"Should I stop seeing him?" she wondered aloud.

"I don't know the answer to that," I replied, "but I think you might have a better chance at making the right decision if he can tell you what he needs."

"At least it's a question that doesn't sound like an attack," she agreed.

After a bit more sniffling and a lot of commiseration, we hung up. I wondered if Steve would be able to say, or if he even knew, what he needed. I surely couldn't have answered that question. I had hopes that, for Tammy's sake, it would at least open the discussion in a civilized way. I also hoped she would meet him in person, and wear that shiny leopard dress.

Dinner with Cheryl and Don was a relaxing barbecue on the canal abutting their backyard. They had also invited Paolo, rounding out our number and taking some of the burden of conversation off of me. We started off with a round of margaritas, lounging in lawn chairs at the edge of the water while Don lit the coals.

"Don is the only person in south Florida who bothers to barbecue on coals," Cheryl said. I couldn't tell if she was complaining or bragging. From where I was sitting I could see into several of the neighbors' backyards, which boasted huge gas grills. Cheryl smiled. "He says it proves that he's not in a hurry. He needs to remind himself that he is retired."

Cheryl looked completely happy and relaxed in a pair of fitted dark pants and a loose white linen tunic. She wore a chunky amber necklace and a simple gold wedding band. I thought about how I would look in that outfit. Old, I thought. But on Cheryl it looked elegant but casual, concealing a body that I knew was trim and muscular. I made a mental note to try this style out in a few dozen years.

An alligator surfaced in the narrow canal. I jumped out of my chair and backed toward the house.

"Don't worry," Don reassured me, "he's just passing through. He's a regular. Everyone in the neighborhood calls him Jerome. I don't know why."

Jerome looked at us and continued on his way. Paolo smiled and gestured to my chair. "Come, Mimi, and tell us about yourself. What are you doing up at the citrus plant? Where are you from? What do you do at home?" I explained, leaving out the more boring details of citrus processing.

"That is wonderful," Paolo commented, "because engineers make the best dancers. They have to think everything through, which slows them down. But once they've got it, they've got it on many levels. You'll come to tango lessons again next week?"

By the time the steaks were cooked, we all knew much more about each other. Don, a retired advertising executive, had moved to Florida only a year and a half earlier. He had met Cheryl at Paolo's tango lessons. Cheryl, whose house it was, had retired from teaching music five years earlier and made the decision to come south only three years ago. Paolo was more mysterious. Describing himself as a "former computer professional turned dance bum," he now seemed to support himself through a dozen hours of tango instruction per week. I mentally did the math, and it really didn't compute.

Dessert was a cross between Swedish cream and mango pudding. It was cool and refreshing and reminded me of the fading summer. The sun had long set and the yard was lit with twinkling lights. I could see strings of lights in backyards up and down the canal.

"Oh yes," said Cheryl, "by next week the gardens on all the canals will be completely lit for Christmas. It's a local tradition. You can even take a boat tour of the lit canals. We do it every year." She looked fondly at Don. Every year. They had been married less than one year. I chuckled. Cheryl looked at me oddly.

"We *will* do it every year," Don explained, "It's the most romantic event in Port Charlotte and we made ourselves a promise to do it every year."

"It was our first date," Cheryl added.

I tried to remember my first date with Andy. I believe we went to the exact same Irish session that we heard most weeks thereafter. It seemed so ordinary, so unromantic next to the twinkling lights of the canals. Our return visits certainly did not seem like celebrations of the first date. Was that what they were for Andy? I didn't think so. Coming to Port Charlotte had broken that pattern for us, and now that it was broken I could see that I had been unhappy with it for some time. I smiled at Cheryl.

"How did you know," I asked her, "that Don was the one for you? I don't mean to be nosy, but you both seem to have decided quickly that you found the right person."

"Well, we just got to know each other," Don explained.

"I found out where Don had been and what he had done, what he still hoped to accomplish in his life, what the important things were for him. And he learned the same about me," Cheryl elaborated, "and of course there was the spark of attraction, and I don't know, it just seemed . . ." she trailed off.

"It seemed like we were heading in the same direction, walking the same path," Don continued, "so we decided to walk it together, that's all."

Paolo was listening intently. I noticed this, but was absorbed in my own thoughts. I never looked at my life as a path, at least not once I was grown. I had worked hard to get through school, get my job, and do it well. Perhaps there was once a path, but now I was at the end of it. I wanted a boyfriend, but aside from lust, I wasn't sure why. Maybe that was the reason they didn't stick around. Jerome surfaced in the canal and disappeared again, taking my thoughts with him.

Walking me to my car, Paolo thanked me for asking Cheryl that question.

"Tango is a beautiful dance," Paolo was saying, "and

I love what I do. But I always wonder how people make these big decisions, like marriage." He looked at me. "I wanted so badly to be a dance teacher, and now I am one. And yet I still wonder what direction I should take next."

"I know," I said, "what's the next step? That's my usual question." I gestured at the cozy house, the lights. "These people, they can see the whole path. I wonder what that would be like."

Paolo opened the door of my car. As I moved to get in, he leaned over and gave me a quick kiss on the forehead.

"For your thoughts," he said, and I drove away.

Tanner called to express his boredom. Since Lu and Schaeffer had left his job site and Ben had arrived to replace them, there had not been a single tale worth telling.

"Maybe I could convince Dan to send Ben to Florida and have you sent up here. Then at least I could follow you around when you go shopping after work. How's the orange juice? How was tango?"

I told Tanner about the state of the factory. Then I tried to cheer him up by describing some of my less successful dance moments with some of my less-than-helpful partners.

"This week I'm considering wearing the steel-toed boots," I teased. I wanted Tanner to think of the possibilities and sing. I was trying to guess what song he might spontaneously choose.

Tanner just sighed. So I told him about the dinner

party at Cheryl and Don's, with an exaggerated description of Jerome. I could hear him perking up slightly.

"And furthermore," I continued, "Paolo said engineers make the best dancers, because they think things through."

This outrageous claim seemed to do the trick. Tanner cleared his throat and sang in a high, girly voice, "Leave them on or take them off!"

"What on earth are you singing?" But he just continued, until he was belting out the phrase "Blue tango shoes!" repeatedly.

"Mist: a Finnish punk rock group. Where have you been?"

Tanner and I used to go out to hear music together. It was a trial for both of us. We gave it up due to irreconcilable differences. Now when we hang out we go to art openings instead.

"Mimi, you should go buy some hot dress to wear to tango class. Maybe you'll meet some rich, handsome guy who will whisk you away from all of this and make you a part of high society in Buenos Aires."

"You and Tammy would have to come with me as wardrobe consultants. I'm not cut out for the part, and I would need a good disguise."

"It would be my pleasure," he assured me, "but I assure you, a sexy tango dress is appropriate any time after dark. Were Cheryl and Don trying to set you up with that fellow Paolo?"

I should not have been surprised. When it comes to

social nuance, Tanner has antennae several feet long. He picks up on every possible implication of any situation, instantly computes the probabilities, and goes straightaway to his favorite scenario. He is worse than Tammy, who at least pretends to exercise caution before passing judgment. I, of course, had wondered this myself. I didn't think so. And the quick kiss Paolo gave me as I got into the car I considered affectionate, nothing more. I changed the subject.

"I don't know about that. But I do know there is no reason for you to be bored."

"Really? In Kannapolis? Do you know that the sign over the highway as you enter town says 'Kannapolis, most boring place on earth'?" Tanner was on a roll. "Ben and I went out looking for some music and, after asking at least ten people, we found a place with a band. They were playing ABBA covers. All night. I couldn't help myself. I started to sing along, and Ben insisted we go back to the hotel. It was a very early evening."

"Listen," I said, "to relieve boredom all you have to do is bring up Lu. Or Schaeffer. Ben had words with both of them the day before they left. I bet there is a story there." I wasn't being nice to Ben. He probably wouldn't enjoy being interrogated by Tanner. But I'm a loyal friend, and Tanner has been known to go to great lengths to avoid boredom. It could get loud.

Extricating myself from the conversation, I called Tammy. I had expected to hear from her much earlier and was quite worried about her. She didn't answer, so I texted a quick "What's up?" and went to bed.

But I couldn't sleep. I kept thinking of that quick, affectionate kiss on my forehead. I tried to concentrate on the last date I had with Andy, which had been lovely. I went over every detail of it in my head. But when I tried to stop thinking and go to sleep, the little kiss intruded again. Finally I managed to control my thoughts and go to sleep by concentrating on the gliding figure of Jerome.

We had pretty good luck all morning, until we came to pump 37. Carlos kept turning it on, but I could never see a change on the monitor. I tried to start it remotely but got no heartbeat back from the system, and Carlos confirmed that it wasn't starting. In most factories like this one, individual devices can be turned on and off by hand. Carlos went off to find the guys who usually tended that part of the plant, while I went out to pump 37 and traced the communications wire back to the computer. I followed it as far as the control room door without finding any breaks or other problems.

Carlos came back to tell me that they had been turning this pump on by hand for the last six months. They never bothered to tell him, they just kept an eye on the situation and turned it on when they thought the vat was getting too full and needed to be emptied. From his station in the control room, Carlos could not tell that the pump was not being activated by the control system. Fortunately, Carlos is very even-tempered.

I had traced the communications line to the large cabinet containing all of the junctions between the various devices and the computer. To figure out what was wrong with pump 37 we would have to trace the line into the cabinet, find the junction box, and see where its outgoing line went. We would have to test the viability of all the lines.

"I don't see how the problem could be in there," he said, "because two years ago we replaced all of the wires in that cabinet."

"We have to look," I replied, "just to rule out the possibility."

I suspected the problem was inside, because the rainstorm that had soaked the main computer had also reached the cabinet. The lock on the door was rusted shut and Carlos went off to find some tools to break it. He came back with a hammer and some other small implements of destruction. He also brought the factory foreman, who was swearing abusively at Carlos for having locked it in the first place. I understood why it was locked: to keep the monkeys out.

I took the tools out of Carlos's hands. If anybody broke anything besides the lock, it was going to be me. I couldn't bear the thought of Carlos listening to endless insults from the foreman. At least I would eventually be gone. The lock was just a regular padlock. I cannot say how many times I have done this. I held it with a vice-grip and easily broke it open with a hammer. The foreman swore at me appreciatively, complimenting my gender as well as my skill.

In addition to all the junctions running from the factory floor into the control room, the cabinet contained about a cubic foot of fluffy packing material. The bottom of the cabinet was covered in a quarter inch of feces. The disgusting smell filled the control room.

"Rats," said Carlos, unnecessarily. My stomach turned upside down and I ran outside. Carlos and the foreman joined me.

The foreman was swearing steadily now. Between bouts of obscenities, I learned that they had paid a company, probably one of our competitors, to replace all of the wires in that cabinet with fiber-optic cables. It now seemed that a sizeable fraction of them were compromised.

"Rats love fiber-optic cable," I explained. "I don't know who talked you into replacing everything, but it wasn't a good idea." Fortunately he hadn't been persuaded to do this by Dan. Through the fog of profanity I heard the familiar complaint that the old system had to be repaired too often. The foreman and his boss had hoped that, by replacing the cabinet full of wires, somehow I wouldn't need to come and fix their factory year after year. Carlos and I both knew the truth. The monkeys would keep me in business forever.

I sighed. "I can rewire it for you with conventional wire and connectors. Or you can send it out to the shop, but better be quick. Then, if the rats get in they won't be likely to eat through the wires. You can also protect it with a layer of hardware cloth. Can you get someone to come clean it out?"

At lunch I gave Carlos my cell phone number.

"If that foreman ever utters a sentence without the word 'fuck' in it, I want you to text me immediately. I just need to know."

Carlos laughed. We were at his favorite Cuban restaurant, ordering *vaca frita* and *maduros*. As we tucked into the hearty meal, he looked at me seriously.

"I told Anna about our conversation the other day," he began, "and she wanted me to ask you some questions."

"Shoot," I said. Carlos had never made me feel uncomfortable before, and I trusted him now.

"What do you want your life to look like ten years from now?" He smiled. It made me think Anna had once asked him this same question, and his answer had made all the difference.

"Well, I guess I never think that far ahead."

"Please do so now," he pushed. I tried to imagine.

"I can't see anything but more of what I already do now. Except maybe some vacations, or some small adventures. I wish I could have an adventure." I thought about my urge to see the Brazilian jungle. Unnervingly, Jerome came to mind.

"I'm not talking about vacations or adventures," prodded Carlos," I am talking about the whole package. What does it look like?"

"I don't know."

"Mimi," Carlos had an air of urgency, "nobody can know this but you. Make it your business to know what you want."

I shrugged. "I'll work on it," I said. And after a moment or two, I remembered, "What is Anna's second question?"

"This boyfriend of yours, what is his name again?"

"Andy."

"When you spend time with Andy, does it make your heart sing?"

I looked at Carlos. I couldn't imagine these words coming out of his mouth or the mouth of any engineer I knew. He did look uneasy. I remembered that this was

Anna's question.

"I don't know," I replied. His response surprised me.

"Fuck, Mimi, how can you not know? What makes you happy? I mean, incredibly, over the top happy? What makes you laugh and love life?"

I thought about this. We ate in silence.

"You know, I'm at my happiest with Tanner and Tammy, both of whom make me laugh. And they both care about me and want the best for me. I love the way they look at life. I guess I've never had a boyfriend who made me feel quite that way. It would be hard for any boyfriend to match them."

"Now, why do you say that?" Carlos looked genuinely shocked.

"I don't know. I've just never met anybody who came close. I always think that I need to get to know the person, but after a few months I realize it's just never going to happen."

Carlos pushed back from the table, rocked slowly in his chair, crossing his arms over his chest.

"Mimi, you need to sharpen your senses. You should be able to tell on the first date."

~~~

"*La Cumparsita.*"

The sociable dancers were helping Paolo decide which tango music was the easiest to follow. They rattled off a list of possibilities, mostly Spanish names. I relaxed with my beer and inhaled the salty air. In spite of monkeys and rats and alligators with formal first names, a week in Port Charlotte had done me a lot of good. It was clearly time to re-evaluate my life and try to steer it a bit. I had been drifting.

"Mimi is the least experienced dancer," Cheryl pointed out, "so she would be the best judge."

Nobody could argue with that assessment of my dancing. Of course, I have danced all my life. But the usual bopping around that happens on a popular dance floor had nothing in common with what they were discussing.

Paolo agreed. He pulled his cell phone out and called up a tune. Putting it on speakerphone, he stood up and offered me his hand. I'm the student, so I obeyed.

Once again I walked backward along the deck. This time he led me right to the far rail, then slowly rocked forward and back, changing direction.

"Give me your weight," he said, putting my left arm higher on his shoulder and pulling my belly tight against his. "Push against me with your body, but don't lean."

We stood like this for a moment, arms loose and limp but braced against each other. Then we began to walk with the music again. As I relaxed a bit, I began to listen to the tune more carefully. It was thumpy and dramatic, impossible to miss the beat. If Elmer Fudd and Bugs Bunny ever did a tango together, rifle in hand, it would have been to this tune. I smiled to myself.

Paolo quickly shifted his feet without giving me a chance to change my weight with him. "Just go with it," he said. I felt my hips swerving to match his step while moving my feet in a straight line: my left foot going backward as his left foot stepped forward. As we approached the table, Don and Cheryl clapped. Paolo released me.

"Your first close embrace," Cheryl explained. I wouldn't have put it that way, exactly. "You are a natural," she added.

"Too bad I only have a few weeks to take lessons here," I said. I realized I would miss it. I would have to look for lessons when I got home, and I wondered if I would like them as much with a different teacher and different friends. Paolo was studying me.

"You could take a few private lessons with me if you would like," he offered, "and when you go back to Boston you could join any tango class with confidence."

The group agreed that this was an excellent idea. I asked how many of them had taken private lessons. Almost everybody had done so at some point and all said they enjoyed it. I got out my date book and showed it to Paolo. The next several weeks consisted entirely of blank pages.

"I think I could make some time," I said. He laughed.

Driving back to my hotel room, I realized that the week had passed and I hadn't heard from Andy once. I wondered what he had done for fun the previous Friday, without our usual dinner and music date. I remembered Tammy and wondered whether she had spoken with Steve or just shut him off entirely. I resolved to make two phone calls. But when I got back to the room, the full exhaustion of the day hit me and I put it off. I showered and crawled under the covers. The phone beeped. It was a text from Tanner:

Greetings, Mimi. You are so right about some things. Lu offered to introduce Ben to her sister. Flipped him out completely. More later. T

I thought it over carefully before dialing. I would start with small pleasantries and ask about his week. I would entertain him with a few stories from work. Then I would ask him one of Anna's questions. I wasn't sure which one.

"Well, I just went to the pub by myself. It was awesome. The piper came early and played two full sets. I sat as close to the music as I could get. You know, they used to scare armies off with those pipes."

I described the cabinet filled with the rat's nest. Andy chuckled. Eventually the moment seemed right.

"Andy," I said, "tell me. Where do you see yourself in ten years? What do you imagine you will be doing?" There was a long pause.

"Why do you ask?"

"Because I've been asking myself this question, and I haven't really got an answer but I thought maybe you would. What do you think?" There was another long pause.

"I guess I see myself doing pretty much what I'm doing now. Is there anything wrong with that?"

"No, of course not," I answered, although I wanted to scream *Yes, everything is wrong with that!*

"There is nothing wrong with your life either," he pointed out, "and no reason to change any of it. You

40

always look completely happy to me. That's one reason I like to spend time with you."

"Thank you," I replied lamely, wondering how to get out of the conversation I had wanted so badly to start.

"Mimi?"

"Yes, dear?"

"Do you think maybe we could see other people?" I sat down. Where was this coming from? His deep contentment with life, so recently revealed? I was afraid to ask.

"I think that might be okay."

"Good, I was hoping you would say that. We'll get together as soon as you get back. Take care, Mimi, see you soon." And with the click of the phone, something inside me popped like a bubble.

This time I was crying on the phone with Tammy. I didn't know if I wanted to be with Andy. I didn't know if he wanted to be with me. But I was sure I didn't want him seeing other people, not while we were together. So why did I agree to it immediately? Tammy would explain it all, I was sure.

"I understand completely," she said. "You are a sequential committer. You don't need a lifetime commitment, but you don't want to share."

The second part of that was surely true. I had discovered that I really and truly did not want to share. Tammy went on.

"That is one of the five main personality types for women. I was just reading about it in *Glamour*." Tammy mainlined pop psychology. "I'm slightly different," she continued, "I'm a reflective nester. I want someone around all the time, sharing my space."

The conversation was not as helpful as I'd hoped. I brought up the subject of Steve.

"Oh, we are fine," she replied.

"But what about the girl at the movies?" Tammy had been so upset the day she'd seen Steve out with someone else, I thought she was going to dump him instantly.

"Oh, we straightened that out," she replied breezily. "He agreed not to see other girls. And it turned out the girl at the theater was his cousin."

Tammy's problems were under control. Mine were not.

"So why did I tell him it was okay?" I wondered aloud.

"Because you love him and are afraid of losing him," she explained. I thought about this. It was an obvious answer.

"No," I said. "Somehow that's not quite it."

"You love him?" she asked. I wasn't sure, but I said nothing. She tried again. "Are you afraid of losing him?" I tried that on and it didn't feel right either.

"You know what?" I said. "I think I was mostly insulted. Since I got here I've had time to think about Andy and I was starting to come to the conclusion that I would be better off with someone else. Who, I can't say."

I told Tammy what Carlos said about the first date.

"I wouldn't go that far," she replied, "but it is true that on my first date with Steve I had the strong sense that we could be a pair for a long time, maybe forever. It just seemed right."

I was no longer angry with Andy. Maybe he had just seen what I saw but couldn't admit it. I was envious of Tammy and her ability to sense immediately that Steve would be a good match for her. No wonder she was a wreck at the thought of him wanting to see anybody else.

"I wish I had your intuition," I said. "I have never had that feeling about anybody. And it's not just that, either. I have the worst time figuring out what other people are thinking, and half the time I can't even see what's going on in front of my nose. I always rely on you and Tanner to fill me in; otherwise I would just blunder along."

Tammy laughed. "You can be dense sometimes," she agreed.

"I need a plan. And I need you to help me."

"Okay," Tammy replied sympathetically, "here's your plan: Do nothing. Let it ride. There's no use insisting on a commitment just so you don't feel insulted. See what he does in the next few weeks. See what you do. Consider yourself free and do what you want. Pay attention to how you feel. Watch what happens. And tell me everything."

Thank heavens for Tammy. I had a plan.

In a private dance lesson there is nowhere to hide. Paolo made me walk around the room, forward and backward, for twenty minutes straight. Sometimes there was music, sometimes not. He made me adjust the way my feet met the floor, the smoothness with which my legs moved, the exact placement of my heels, the bend of my knees. He made me tuck in my buns, open my chest, drop my shoulders. All of these directions were interspersed with injunctions to relax.

"Relax, Mimi," he was saying, "and don't crane your neck. Push your head toward the ceiling. Why are you laughing?"

"Because you started at my feet and now you're on my head. I'm hoping you will run out of advice soon!"

Paolo laughed. "No, I'll just start over with the feet." He could see I was getting a little frustrated. He turned off the music and stood facing me.

"Come to me and put your upper body against mine." Only a dance instructor could say this with a straight face. I laughed again, but he just looked at me. I walked up until we were touching.

"Now push against me, but without leaning or losing balance." This was harder. I tried to follow his instructions, but he told me I was leaning. "No," he said, "push. Bend your knees a bit and push upward against me. Good, that's better."

Paolo took my right hand in his left, and put his right arm around me with his hand securely pressed in the center of my back. He moved forward and I moved with him, trying to remember all of the things we had just gone over. I sought the floor with my heels. I stepped in a straight line. I dropped my shoulders. I pushed my head toward the ceiling.

"You have lost the connection," Paolo chided.

"I was trying not to stick out my butt," I explained. He laughed and put on some music. Around and around the floor we moved, with fewer instructions than before. Still, I was constantly corrected by small adjustments from his hands, his weight. He started to vary the speed of his steps, sometimes slow, sometimes twice to the beat. I had little trouble following him.

"Don't anticipate. Wait for my lead." We continued walking until it began to feel smooth. Tango is basically walking, but that description is misleading. It's two people walking together, moving as smoothly as the front and back ends of a cat. The same cat.

"Close your eyes. Keep the connection."

I had never danced with closed eyes before. Relying completely on Paolo's touch, the movement became something entirely different. I became aware of slight changes in the direction of his body, of shifts in his weight, and tiny variations in his hands. I would not have noticed these things with my eyes open. The connection between us became the key. Without it, I would have been just standing there with my eyes shut.

We took a break. I could feel my thighs burning a bit from the exertion. Normally people walk by falling. An ordinary walker is an inverted pendulum, falling onto each foot and pushing off into an arc over it. But despite its similarities to walking, the tango was more about balance. Balance on the left foot, reach backward and seek the floor with the right. Then step onto the right foot and balance again. It was a lot of work. Paolo fetched two glasses of water.

"Mimi, you are good. It may not seem like it, but you are catching on much more quickly than most people." He smiled at me as I rubbed my legs, which were starting to cramp. "Engineers make the best dancers!"

I smiled.

"However," he said seriously, "you will be sore tomorrow."

"That's okay," I replied.

"It had better not stop you from coming to the group lesson."

"Oh no," I assured him, "I'll be there."

As we continued the lesson, Paolo gradually increased the variation in his steps, sometimes moving backward, sometimes to the side. Whenever I missed a cue he just corrected me with his hands and his weight, occasionally admonishing me to "keep the connection." My eyes remained closed. I was almost dancing in a dream. It stopped feeling like a lesson.

"There," he said, bringing the lesson to a close. "How did that feel?"

I hesitated.

"Well," I said honestly, "it reminded me of dreaming. It was . . ." I hesitated. "Seductive."

Paolo looked hard at me, then at his shoes.

"Perhaps you already know," he said quietly, "that is the origin of the tango." He looked at me again, with a mischievous twinkle in his eyes.

"Would you like to have dinner?"

Consider yourself free and do what you want. Pay attention to how you feel. Watch what happens. Tammy's words rose in my head. How did I feel about this new development? The words came unbidden from my mouth.

"I'd be delighted."

"That is the third time this person has called me. I have no idea who it is, and I always have my hands full when it happens. I can't deal with it now."

I put the phone back in my purse and went back to my shrimp. Carlos and I had escaped to a seafood place near the plant for a quick lunch. We were making progress. Every device the computer was supposed to track showed a heartbeat. I could see all of them now. The next step was to reprogram the animation so that the heartbeats were all shown in the correct places. The last step would be to make sure that the numerical readouts were calibrated correctly. We would test them one by one and compare readings from the instruments with those shown on the computer display. It would be tedious but straightforward.

Carlos cleared his throat.

"I want to apologize, Mimi."

"For what?" Carlos had never done anything requiring an apology.

"For all of the swearing." I understood. He was apologizing on behalf of the plant manager.

"Oh, don't worry," I assured him, "There are plenty worse than him out there."

"And also the way he insulted you this morning."

47

Now Carlos was apologizing because earlier the plant manager had complimented me on my work thus far, while simultaneously making rude comments about the presence of "girls," as he put it, in factories.

"He is a product of his environment," I generously offered, adding "and also a dinosaur. Don't worry about him. It's the standard engineering thing."

"He creates a bad environment," Carlos said heatedly, "and it's not standard at all. I never heard anyone else speak like that. I can't imagine where it comes from or why he thinks it's okay."

This time I looked at Carlos like he was from another, much nicer, planet.

"Where did you go to school?"

This, it turned out, explained it all. Carlos went to a public university in Miami while living at home with his parents. From there he took this job, having already married his sweetheart, Anna. So he missed the songs.

"Carlos," I explained, "in the Northeast and most other parts of the country people don't live with their parents when they go to the big fancy schools. All the future engineers are in dorms together—dorms filled with boys. And these boys, when they are not thinking about engineering, are thinking about exactly two other things: alcohol and women."

"Okay," Carlos said, laughing, "that seems normal. But it doesn't explain abusive behavior."

"So, for example," I continued, "they go out on weekends and get drunk and sing songs. When I was in college I heard all the songs—usually parodies of old folk tunes or popular music. Even the professors sometimes referred to the songs in class, as a joke. I can sing you a dozen songs about engineers, women, and alcohol. In these songs, not one engineer is a woman, of course, and the guys in the songs get laid in every single verse. Except the verses strictly about beer."

"Really?" Carlos was indeed from another planet.

"I think it warps their minds. It certainly doesn't improve their politeness." I leaned over and quietly sang a verse of an old favorite.

> *A maiden and an engineer were sitting in the park,*
> *The engineer was working on some research after dark,*
> *His scientific method was a marvel to observe,*
> *While his right hand held the figures, his left hand traced*
> *the curves.*

I watched for the reaction. It was mild. I continued.

> *Godiva was a lady well-endowed there is no doubt,*
> *She never wore a stitch of clothes, just wound her hair*
> *about,*
> *The first man who did make her was an engineer, of*
> *course,*
> *But on just one beer an artsie queer had made Godiva's*
> *horse.*

Carlos frowned. I went on to make my point.

> *Late one night, an engineer was lost in work and toil,*
> *He set off to find a darling girl to help discharge his coil.*
> *In no time at all he'd warmed her up, her resistance at a*
> *low...*
> *They fluxed until the morning's light, when their fuses, they*
> *did blow.*

Carlos hung his head.

"I was hoping my daughter would go into engineering. I thought maybe she would grow up to be like you. She wants to go to the Northeast for college. How much of this stuff is out there?" he asked.

A man sitting two tables away turned and looked at us. He appeared to be dressed for a fishing trip, and looked like he could be retired. I thought he was going to complain about my singing. After all, the lyrics were marvelously crude. Instead he smiled.

"MIT man myself," he said.

Carlos looked at me in disbelief. I shrugged, smiling. My phone rang again and I ignored it.

"Let's go back to work. I need to leave by six. I'm taking tango lessons in Port Charlotte."

Carlos shook his head and smiled at me.

"I hope she does grow up to be like you."

"I have been trying to reach you for two days!" The unmistakable voice of Ljudmila Dineva rang in my ears. So this was the mystery caller.

"Hi, Lu, how's it going?"

Dan had given Lu the task of designing the graphics for a new installation. Her job was to take the diagrams of the factory process and turn them into animations that would eventually be connected to all of the devices that reported to, or were controlled by, the main computer. According to Lu, she was having no problem with this. I asked what prompted her to call.

"Dan and a few of the other senior engineers want to review my work. I'm almost sure it is fine. I think I've done everything the customer wanted. But I wanted Schaeffer to look at it first, and he's out of town! And I wanted you to look at it, too, and you're gone. I just don't want to be picked to pieces. Some of these guys are out for me, I just know it."

Lu was, in my opinion, paranoid. I wondered what songs the Bulgarian boy engineers sang. I decided to give her the benefit of the doubt.

"I can log in remotely and look at it, but not until ten tonight. Give me the password to your computer."

"Can't you do it now?" She was getting whiny.

I thought about my tango class. I thought about dinner with Paolo and the second sweet little kiss that ended the evening. Pay attention, I thought to myself, to how you feel.

"Sorry, I have another commitment until then. Just get in early tomorrow and you will have an email from me with comments. I really have to run now." And with some effort, I got her off the phone.

Tango class was fun, and I found I was already much better at it. But an evening out is not as much fun when you know you have to get back and do a few hours of work. I had to turn down a chance to go out for a drink with the group. I pulled Paolo aside and explained the situation. He seemed to understand. I made a date for another private lesson. He suggested the very next day, to be followed by dinner. I was, once again, delighted.

I spent two hours checking the details of Lu's graphics against the scanned factory diagram. Her work was fine. In fact, it was better than fine, and I told her so.

Sometimes my social antennae work quite well and I can see into the future. It astonishes me when this happens, but it rarely makes me happy. Lu will present her work to the guys and they will see that it is good. They will be surprised, and they will show it. And she will take their surprise as an insult, which it surely will be.

"It looked like her granny sewed her right into her jeans." They had sent Tanner back to the office, just in time to witness Lu's presentation.

"Were the graphics good?" I wanted to know that Lu's work was appreciated.

"Who could tell? Nobody but me could take their eyes off her ass."

"But you could, right?" I pointed out. "So tell me how it went."

"Girl, I *am* telling you how it went. I can't believe anybody heard a word she said." This was annoying. At exactly the moment people needed to realize that Lu was doing good, independent work, nobody was listening. Tanner went on.

"She was wearing this loose, low-cut blouse that looked like it might fall off any minute. The suspense was almost too much to bear. And then there were the bracelets, about ten of them stacked up on one arm, jangling around when she gestured. You should have seen the look on Dan's face."

Now I was worried. I got off the phone and called Dan.

"What's the problem, Mimi?" he inquired.

"No problems here at all," I replied, "but I know Lu was working hard on that graphics program and I wanted to hear how her presentation went, if you don't mind."

"Oh!" Dan was a little surprised. We don't usually check up on each other this way. "It was fine. In fact, her graphics program was as good as anybody's, which is high praise for such a new hire. I was really happy with it."

Tanner does like to exaggerate a situation, but I wanted to be sure.

"Can I ask you something? Sometimes people get distracted by Lu's, um, clothes. I was just hoping they didn't get in the way of things."

Dan laughed. "Oh yes, many people were extremely distracted, especially the younger guys. But Mimi," and here he paused for emphasis, "you have to remember that I am the father of three teenage girls. I've had my shots. When I see Lu all tricked out in her tight pants—and yes, they were extremely tight—it just reminds me of the kids. I hope my girls can do such a good job when their turn comes."

"Will you do me a favor?" I rarely asked for favors from Dan.

"Of course."

"Please tell her that you liked her work." He seemed surprised at the request, but agreed.

I thanked Dan and got off the phone, sighing with relief. Then I got ready for my evening of tango and dinner. Carlos said I should be able to tell on the first date whether someone was a keeper. I wasn't sure if a lesson counted as a date, even if there was dinner afterward. But I wasn't going to take any chances.

I ironed the sheer navy blouse and the flouncy skirt and put on tights and high heels. I thought of Lu and put on more jewelry than usual and some light perfume. No jeans this time. Dress for the date you want.

After holding me close for an hour and a half while I moved mostly backward, Paolo made me dinner. We went to his little house at the end of a cul de sac, and he slid a dish into the oven to bake. Then he opened some wine, put out some cheese, and we relaxed while the dinner cooked.

I had assumed that Paolo was from Italy. He had a soft accent and an Italian name. But as we talked I found out that he was from Corsica but had been in the U.S. since college. He had only become a citizen a few years earlier, although he had worked in the states continuously for a dozen years.

"What did you do before teaching tango?" I only knew his description of himself as a former computer professional. That could mean many things. I wondered if it was a sore spot, and gave him a way out. "You don't have to tell me, but I was curious."

"Well, most people I meet when I teach tango wouldn't be interested, but maybe you would. I was teaching computer science and doing research in cryptology. I developed a cipher, or rather, a series of ciphers, that were useful for protecting information transfer on the Internet. My university sought a patent, and I started a business. It was a windfall, really."

"So you quit teaching?"

"Not immediately. But I had to take a leave in order to deal with the consequences of the patent, which amounted to starting a business. And the business did very well. I could have just continued in my academic job. They certainly wanted me to stay, and there is something appealing about being the distinguished professor." Paolo smiled.

"How did you ever end up here?"

"Well, after the money started coming in regularly and I had plenty stashed away in investments, I decided it was time to review my life. What did I really want to be doing and where did I see myself in three years? In ten? And I realized my life was unbalanced. I liked to do research but I didn't need the university for that. I liked to teach but not necessarily computer science, not necessarily undergraduates. I hated giving grades. I did not care for my location."

"Where was that?"

"Boston."

"And you chose Port Charlotte instead?"

"Not exactly. I could run my business from anywhere. But I decided my life was lacking in three ways. One was a lack of music and another was the lack of physical movement. I decided to combine these. I tried many forms of dance, but the tango, as you once said, is seductive. I decided to become good at it, to master it, and to become a teacher. I trained in several places. I started in Boston, then found a great teacher in Atlanta, and finally spent six months in Buenos Aires. After a few years I felt I could begin to teach others properly."

"You changed your life's path entirely."

"Yes, and it was a good thing. I have a more balanced life now. In retrospect, I could have stayed at the university and still done all of these things. But I couldn't see that at the time."

"What was the third thing you lacked?"

At this, Paolo hesitated, embarrassed.

"Company. A partner. Not just a dance partner, I mean. And for a while I thought I had found her. She was a dancer and a graduate student near here, in Tampa. I moved here to be near her. Unfortunately, it did not work out. But I started teaching and now I've built up a clientele, so to speak. I know it's time to re-evaluate my situation again. But I've gotten lazy about it."

Dinner was served. We ate Paolo's homemade stew of veal with olives and we talked some more, late into the night. I had to pull myself away to be ready for work the next day. Once again, he walked me to my car. As he opened the door, I turned to him. He responded, exactly as I had hoped. When he finally released me, I was too flustered to say goodnight. Instead I blurted out, "I'm so sorry you don't like Boston!" and drove off, happy and miserable at the same time.

I had been up too late. I was sleepy and sullen, facing a computer monitor full of information that I understood the day before. Now it was incomprehensible. I peered at it through the fog that always settled on me after too many glasses of wine. I drank a third cup of coffee. I hate working Saturdays.

Usually they don't want outside contractors at the plant on weekends. But this job was dragging on and now there was a sense of urgency about things. Time, tide, and ripening fruit wait for no man. The first truckloads of oranges were due to arrive by the end of the week.

Carlos was off for the weekend, and another guy had been assigned to help me out. He was on the plant floor with his half of the two-way radio, turning stuff off and on while I checked that the right item on the monitor responded. Sometimes engineering is creative and exciting. Sometimes it is boring as hell. In my current state, this tedious task was about all I could handle.

It almost took my mind off Paolo. I wondered what would have happened if I didn't need to go to work today. We had a few passionate moments, which surely would have turned into something more. I thought about his kisses, the warmth of his embrace. I couldn't help it.

"Miss Miranda, are you there?" The radio interrupted the fantasy forming in my head. "I just turned on siphon 42, do you see it?"

"I'm looking." And now I was indeed looking. "Yes, here it is. It's fine. What have you got next?"

If I were not at work I might be having coffee with Paolo, maybe walking on a sandy beach, maybe holding hands. We could have spent the day together, going for a bike ride or renting a kayak and exploring the mangroves.

"Miss Miranda, temperature sensor 56, do you see it?"

On the other hand, the only reason I was still here at all was that the job was going slowly—oh, so slowly. There was no way I could make it slower and it would be done in a week. What then?

"Miss Miranda, siphon 33."

"You can call me Mimi. I see it. It's good."

I tried to avoid thinking about anything romantic

whatsoever. It didn't work. I tried to imagine Paolo as a long-term friend, an acquaintance I would dance with for a few weeks each November. I could not avoid paying attention to my feelings around that idea.

"What's wrong, Mimi?" the voice at the other end of the radio went on: "pump 12?" I had started to cry.

"Something in my eye," I lied. "That one is fine."

I was grateful Carlos wasn't there to go to lunch. I was a complete mess, and in no mood for socializing. I bought a tuna sandwich at the mini-mart and ate in the car. The sooner I went back to work, the less thinking I was likely to do. At least that is what I told myself. Before returning to work I checked my cell for messages. Reception was terrible inside the plant.

And there it was: a text from Paolo.

Dinner again, please? Will pick you up at 7.

Yes, of course. I'd be delighted. Oh, yes, yes!

I told the foreman I had to take Sunday off to do my laundry and write a report for Dan. A blue string of complaints filled the control room. I stood my ground, pointing out that over half the factory was now ready to respond to the control panel and, as they start up only one centrifuge per day until all are running, there would be plenty of time to get them all on line before they were needed. The foreman reluctantly cursed in agreement. I was free!

Two things absolutely needed to happen before dinner. I ran a bath and called Tammy. As soon as she picked up I started to cry again. I knew that would happen. It was best to get it all out well in advance of seeing Paolo again. I filled her in on details of the last two weeks.

"You've been having an adventure! That's wonderful." Tammy sometimes had the strangest way of looking at things. "Just take it as it comes. Don't assume it can't work out."

"But it can't work out!" I told her about his life and how he actually preferred this little town, which might as well have been a gated retirement community, to the vibrancy of Boston.

"And I don't have anything to wear," I added. Everything was dirty except my jeans, and they weren't exactly clean. This was one reason I needed to talk to Tammy.

"So wear the jeans. They go with everything. Is the blue shirt clean? Good. What have you got to go under it? What kind of underwear did you bring? Take the underwear seriously."

I found my laciest underwear, washed it in the sink, and used the blow dryer on it for fifteen minutes. Tammy continued to coach me on shoes and accessories.

"Do not take that bag of yours. It's a computer bag, for god's sake. Just stuff your credit card and phone in your coat pocket. Leave the key at the desk. Next time you go on a job I'm going to help you pack. It wouldn't be that hard to bring a dress."

"I did pack a dress! You made me, remember? But I've been out dancing and socializing and even that needs a wash."

"Okay." Tammy considered the situation.

"Tomorrow you do laundry and go shopping. You need another outfit."

"If I do laundry, I'll have enough to get through the next week. I'll be okay."

"He'll think you hardly have any clothes!"

"Tammy," I reminded her, "I'm in a hotel room at night and a factory during the day. I don't have many clothes because I don't need them."

"Make an effort," Tammy admonished. "It won't kill you."

Paolo opened the car door for me and then blocked my way. "Let's start the evening right," he said, pulling me close. He kissed me tenderly, stroking my hair. There was no doubt in my mind how the evening would end. My toes curled with pleasure.

We didn't drive into town. To my surprise, Paolo hopped on the freeway and headed south. We got off in Fort Myers and worked our way through the stop-and-go traffic of the town. He wouldn't say where we were going. He drove across the long causeway to Sanibel Island and found parking at the beach.

"I thought a walk and some fresh air would do us both good," he explained, taking my hand. Together we walked for miles down the sandy beach littered with seashells. I laughed and told him about a small piece of my daydream that morning, in which I had the day off and we took a walk on the beach. I explained what I was doing at the plant and why I had to work on the weekend.

"Do you like your job?" It was his turn to question me.

"You know, usually I would say I do. But the last two weeks have been unusual. Amazing, really, with the tango lessons and the company." I looked at him closely. "Work has been mundane in comparison."

"Excellent!" Paolo smiled, drawing me close for another kiss, "I'm glad to be a distraction for you."

Keep it light, I thought. So I told him about the plant, the rats, the swearing foreman. I mentioned that I would probably be returning to Boston at the end of the next week.

"Will you be here on Friday?"

"Definitely. Saturday is the earliest I would leave."

"Do me a favor, Mimi." Paolo gave me a squeeze. "Whatever else happens this week, please save Friday night for me. I have a special treat in mind for you. And try not to leave too early on Saturday, okay?"

We stayed on the island all evening. We walked until we were tired, then found an ocean-front bar. We ordered conch fritters and drinks served with little plastic mermaids decorating the glasses. A magnificent sunset decorated the sky. After dinner we stood with our feet in the water and kissed.

Driving back, Paolo looked at me.

"I don't want to take you to the hotel," he said frankly. "I want to take you home with me."

"I'm not working tomorrow," I said, smiling. This is the bittersweet way of life. Some wonderful things are not going to last forever, or even for a while. So if it is short, let's keep it as sweet as possible. Tammy's words floated to the surface. Let it ride. See what he does. See what you do. Consider yourself free. Pay attention to how you feel. Watch what happens.

CHAPTER 3

Watching the clothes go around in the dryer, I went over everything in my head. I was falling in love, and I should have known that would happen on the first date. I think I did know, but refused to admit it to myself. One point scored for Carlos. On the other hand, the whole affair was futile. It was moving fast, and I knew that I was rushing headlong down a dead end road, with a brick wall at the end of it for brakes. The metaphor did not please me.

My cell rang. It was Tanner.

"Can you pick me up at the airport?"

"Tanner, I'm in Port Charlotte, remember?"

"The Fort Myers airport. The plant requested additional help because they're afraid the work might not be done by Friday."

"Of course it will. I'm expecting to be done by Thursday, but I'll stay until Friday just to make sure there are no problems. You don't need to come."

"I'm already here. Can you pick me up?"

Growling, I pulled the damp clothes from the dryer and threw them into my laundry bag, heading out the door. It was a long ride to the airport and back, meaning I would be late for dinner with Paolo, would have to ditch Tanner at the hotel, and would be wearing clothes that were either wet or dirty or both. I called Paolo and explained the situation. He laughed and insisted that Tanner come to dinner with us.

"I love you," I said unthinkingly.

"Careful," he warned.

The force of our attraction to each other, the intensity of our lust, and the hopelessly short time frame of our affair were working some kind of alchemy on our basic friendship. Instead of holding back, we were pouring forth. Paolo needed to experience as much of my life as he could while I was still here. I could see from his perspective that Tanner presented an opportunity.

I just told him I loved him! In a different context it would have been a terrifying thing to hear or say. But for us, right now, it was just the logical consequence of that first little kiss. "For your thoughts," he had said. Now he had them.

Tanner, I realized, would have to be taken firmly in hand. Riding back from the airport, he gossiped endlessly about people at work.

"So Schaeffer and Ben both got back this week, and there hasn't been a dull moment since. Schaeffer keeps trying to corner Ben and have some kind of discussion about something—I'm sure it's Lu—and Ben hides in his office. Schaeffer and Lu arrive and leave together. According to Jen, the gal we just hired to cover the front desk, she hasn't changed her address or anything, but . . ."

"You are one nosy neighbor," I protested.

"Shall I stop?" Tanner knew better.

"No, go on. But be nice about it. And I also have something to tell you."

"Oh, it can all wait. We have all week. But what did you do to piss off the plant manager? None of us thought you really needed help."

"I took today off. The guy has ants in his pants because we are going to finish our part of the work close to the startup deadline. But it's their own damn fault. They move stuff around and never make a record of it. And they had more monkeys than usual creating chaos this year. And then there were the rats." And I gave him the full story.

"No wonder you said you had something to tell me," he conceded.

"Yes, but that wasn't it."

"Oh?" Now I had Tanner's full attention. I had to come clean.

"I'm having a hot affair with my tango teacher."

Tanner bit his lip and then started, involuntarily, to laugh. He rolled down the window and screamed, "Tango lady! So forbidden, my tango love!"

"Shut up!" I laughed. "And what the heck is that?"

"Rocketbug," he said, "Don't tell me you've never heard of them."

"I've heard of them now. Please, get it out of your system."

"Whatever do you mean by that, Mimi dearest?"

"Because we are going to dinner and you're coming with us. And then I'll likely drop you off at the hotel and be back in the morning to pick you up."

"Mary mother of God," said Tanner piously. "What has happened to our little girl?"

"Prepare"—I looked at him sideways—"to be entertained."

Paolo picked both of us up at the hotel. Tanner wore a crisp blue shirt, freshly ironed, and dark jeans with his favorite Harley Davidson brass belt buckle and a red wool sweater thrown over his shoulders. He looked sharp. I managed to dry my clean underwear with the hair dryer, but had to settle for dirty pants and a slightly damp t-shirt. Everything else was draped around my room, drying.

Paolo looked at Tanner, then at me. I explained my laundry issues. Tanner grinned conspiratorially at Paolo.

"Let's take her shopping." And off we went to the mall, despite my protests. Except for Tanner, I hate shopping with men.

"Don't you think she needs a tango dress?" Tanner asked Paolo. Stuffing all six feet four of Tanner in the back seat did not suppress him in the least.

"Of course!" To his credit, Paolo was enjoying the whole scene enormously. I was beginning to see the potential for an excellent evening. I had obviously lost control of the situation and was at the mercy of forces far beyond my control. Let it ride.

Every store in the mall had a stuffed chair in it, placed strategically for husbands to nap in while their wives shopped. I sat in the husband chair and watched Tanner and Paolo critique an entire rack of dresses.

"Striking," declared Tanner, pulling out a gauzy tea length royal purple item with sequins, "Angelina Jolie on the red carpet."

"Looks like it might fall off her shoulders when she moves. A tango dress has to be secure. Also I wonder if we could get her to wear it."

"We'll just hide her other clothes."

"Right."

"Ooh, here's a nice one." Tanner pulled out a stretchy red dress with a flare skirt.

"Hmm!" Paolo seemed to like it. I found it a bit scary. It looked like something Lu might wear on a date with Schaeffer. Or someone far, far more sophisticated than Schaeffer. Except that it was many sizes larger than anything Lu had ever, or would ever, own.

"She could dress it down for dinner with a short jacket." Tanner wandered over to a rack of jackets. He came back with four of them. I took the jackets and the four dresses they had chosen into the changing room, with instructions to come out in each of them and try on every single jacket.

"Too low cut." I knew that.

"Makes her hips look wide, which they aren't!" Be

careful, boys.

"Nice cut. Let's see the back." Two guys are studying my bum!

"Not sure about the color on her." It made me look jaundiced.

"Ha, she's a fall, except in winter, when she's a spring." Tanner reads too many women's magazines.

Normally having two men analyze how clothes looked on my body would have been a source of painful embarrassment. But Tanner was humorous about it, even reasonably gentle. And after so many hours of tango instruction, with every detail of my body scrutinized, I could hardly mind Paolo's comments.

As soon as the two of them agreed, I declared the venture a success and took my fancy new dress and coat to the register. I thought of Tammy, buying the shiny leopard dress to please Steve. Today I would please two men with one dress. The sales lady, who had been watching the whole process, gave me a bemused look.

"What's the occasion?"

Tanner and I exchanged a glance.

"My other clothes are dirty," I explained simply. We left, Paolo and Tanner stifling their laughter in the sleeves of their shirts.

Over dinner, Tanner regaled us with tales of the office. "So Lu tried to smooth things over and make peace by telling Ben that he was such a nice guy that she wanted to introduce him to her sister. This may have been a tactical error."

I remembered Tanner's text message about this. I hadn't really had time to think about it, but now Ben's behavior was beginning to make sense. She had put him in a position where there was no right response. He could say yes and look like a fool or say no and insult two women. Poor Ben! No wonder he was hiding.

"Then I pissed him off by buying him a Bulgarian-English dictionary. The man has no sense of humor."

I covered my mouth with the starched linen napkin. We were at the best restaurant in Port Charlotte, and still I was overdressed. But it would do no good to blow the oysters Rockefeller right out my nose. Tanner saw how close he had come to making me do exactly that, and grinned wickedly. Paolo watched our interaction closely. He saved me by changing the subject.

"Where did you get your unusual first name?"

"I don't have an unusual first name!" Tanner insisted. Tanner hates his actual first name. Paolo looked at him and waited. Tanner surrendered.

"My name is John Tanner Smith," he explained. "Tanner is my mother's maiden name. Do you know how many people are named John Smith? People don't even believe that's your name. No one will take a credit card with the name John Smith on it. I certainly wouldn't. So I go by Tanner, in order to avoid an identity crisis."

An overdesigned salad arrived, adorned with little curls of some red vegetable and spears of something yellow sticking up. A pinkish dressing glazed the greens and the whole affair sat on a plate drizzled with a sweet brownish sauce.

"I ordered the house salad," I explained to the waiter.

"And this is it, Madame," he replied, smirking slightly. I had the feeling my comment was not unusual. Tanner leaned over and studied my plate. The waiter slid away.

"I bet he doesn't even know what's in it," Tanner clucked. "Looks like sliced radicchio, maybe some raspberry vinaigrette, could be a balsamic reduction on the plate. I wonder what the yellow things are. Ah, well, taste and see."

I looked at Paolo encouragingly. A romantic evening was difficult to achieve with Tanner along.

"Mimi," Paolo said, smiling, "are all of your colleagues as charming as this one? It is no wonder you tell me you like your job."

"And you haven't even heard him sing. But Tanner, tell me some more about Lu and Schaeffer, now that I've recovered from the last revelation. And is there really a sister somewhere? This is the first I've heard about a sister." I turned to Paolo. "Tanner always knows more about office gossip than he lets on, and he has ways of finding things out that, frankly, make me blush. But I've learned that it pays to interrogate."

Tanner laughed. Instead of answering, he pulled out his cell and brought up a photo. Two dark-haired beauties smiled at the camera. On the left was Lu, wearing a furry red jacket over some sparkling beaded thing. On the right was someone slightly taller than Lu, but equally thin, in a green silk blouse with a floral scarf and several necklaces. The face, although a little rounder and fuller, appeared to have been pressed from the same classic mold. Paolo looked at the picture, too.

"Which one is the engineer?" he asked.

"Actually, both," Tanner replied. "Lu's sister just got her work visa. Fortunately, she works in a completely different field. I don't know what would happen if they both worked at our company. Lu brought her by last week, ostensibly to show her the office. All very innocent, of course. Ben made some excuse that he needed an electrical part we didn't have and escaped. But not before Lu managed to introduce him to Tsvetanka."

"I can just imagine!" I was close to having an attack of laughter. "Ben, let me introduce my brilliant, beautiful, and completely harmless sister! Nice to meet you, I have to run now to Home Depot and buy some electrical tape, as we only have two dozen rolls left!"

Tanner was giggling. "Mimi, you are so off the mark here," he said teasingly. "Lu actually introduced her as charming and clever, and never even mentioned the word *harmless*. And Ben claimed to be off to purchase a box of display lights. We only have two cases of those on hand presently. All of the other guys went to lunch with Tsvetanka and pronounced her a delightful lady."

Paolo studied the picture further and sighed. "Marriage," he said, "leads to citizenship. Consider your firm under siege."

We left Tanner off at the hotel and returned to Paolo's apartment. As we drove away we could hear him singing.

"Make it in the moonlight, ochos in the night!" he wailed, his voice carrying across the parking lot as I hurried to the exit. Paolo burst out laughing.

"Pinneo!" he exclaimed. "Blue Tango. I put it in a dance mix once and everyone over fifty turned bright red."

"I can totally understand that," I replied, already bright red.

"Mimi," Paolo continued, "I really do have to ask you something—in fact, a lot of things. Mr. John Tanner Smith is a delight, no doubt. But I sense there are things you want from life besides this" — and here Paolo struggled to say the right thing—"career. Which is a fine career and all, but do you see yourself doing this same thing in ten years?"

There was that question again. And it came out of the mouth I was hoping to kiss shortly. I turned even redder.

"I don't know!" I didn't want to cry, but it wasn't looking good.

"Ah, I've upset you," Paolo looked worried. "I didn't mean to do that."

We rode in silence for a few minutes. "I do like my work," I finally said. "It's not enough, whatever enough may turn out to be. But it is part of who I am—I enjoy solving problems and fixing stuff so that it works. I don't know what else I'd rather do to make a living. It's the non-job part that I need to sort out."

Paolo thought about this.

"Why didn't you like Boston?" I asked, hoping to change the subject. After all, I had a few questions of my own that needed answers.

"It's hard to explain," Paolo said thoughtfully. "I

didn't like the obvious class distinctions. I was put off by the weather, although that was not the biggest deal. When I started to dance, I found the community a bit stuffy. Reasonably welcoming, but rigid. And many years at the same job caused me to be in a bit of a rut. It's as though I had built a box for myself, gotten into it, and nailed it shut. I had to break it open."

We arrived at the house and Paolo took my hand, leading me inside. He put on some music and took me in his arms.

"I want to dance with you while you are still in this gorgeous dress. I don't know if Tanner and I can ever get you to wear it again, but it is delicious."

We danced counterclockwise, revolving slowly around the dining room table.

"If you could take a month off and go anywhere, do anything, where would you go?" This was an easier question, one whose answer had come to me unbidden many times already.

"Brazil," I said, without hesitation.

At that, Paolo kissed me and our evening began to unfold in the most seductive way.

"How delightful to see you!" Carlos welcomed Tanner warmly. "Mimi has been doing an excellent job, but I'm glad to see you all the same."

The factory foreman was less tactful. Through a fog of *fuck*-laced invectives and general insults to both Carlos and me, he expressed a dim sort of gratitude for Tanner's presence.

"Arrive late and take all the credit," Tanner agreed cheerfully. "Happy to oblige."

Truckloads of oranges had begun to arrive—earlier than expected—and several of the centrifuges were in operation. Work at the plant was coming to a close, and Tanner was hastening the end of this job and my time with Paolo. I had promised him I would stay until the following Saturday, but I would perhaps have to take some time off to do it. Dan would go along with it and Tanner would back me up. At lunch we went to Tanner's favorite place, right along the river.

"So," Tanner looked at Carlos, "has Mimi apprised you of her latest, greatest boyfriend?"

Damn, I thought, *I should have seen this coming.*

"This man, Andy," Carlos replied, "but I sense he is not right for our Mimi. Tanner, you need to watch over this lady and make sure she finds someone nice."

"Sir Andy of the bagpipe sessions?" Tanner teased. "He is so yesterday. Oh no, she has met someone quite special right here in Port Charlotte."

Upon seeing the look of astonishment on Carlos's face, Tanner sang, "My baby she can take a chance, my baby got a brand new dance!"

Carlos, stupefied, looked at me. I shrugged. "Just following your advice, actually."

Carlos appeared to be horrified at the thought of someone following his advice.

"Well, actually, it was more Tammy's advice. She said I should relax, let it ride, and see what happens."

"Whooee," agreed Tanner, "something is certainly happening. And the ride looks good, too." Tanner can be difficult to ignore, but I did my best.

"You said," and here I looked at Carlos, "that I should know if someone is right on the first date. And I did, so I acted on that."

"So you will move here? He will go to Boston? You will come and visit a lot? I don't understand how this is going to work out." Carlos looked genuinely concerned.

"It's not going to work out." As soon as the words left my mouth I understood two things. First: it really isn't going to work out. Second: I am now too upset to go back to work.

By the time we got back to the plant, I was having a full blown crack-up fit, with Tanner clucking like a mother hen and Carlos trying to look invisible. They readily agreed to make my excuses to the boss, and sent me home to my little hotel room to be miserable by myself. On the way I stopped at the mini-mart and bought a quart of milk and a large box of cookies. It just seemed like the right thing to do.

Unfortunately, some things cannot be fixed with milk and cookies, a hot bath, or a nap. You can do all these things, as I did, but the broken thing is still broken when the nap is over and the cookies are gone.

"Where are you?" the text message came around six in the evening, from Paolo. He would be with the dancers, on the dock, enjoying a beer and the sunset.

And "Are you ok? Sorry for poking your sore spot." Another text, this time from Tanner. I guess he found a way back to the hotel without my help. I had the car.

And "Great news! Engaged!" from Tammy. Good for her, I thought, with a sudden urge for more milk and cookies.

I decided to ignore them all. A half hour later there was knocking at the door. I figured it was Tanner and I would have to give him the car keys so he could get dinner. When I opened the door, there stood Tanner and Paolo. Before I could react, Tanner stepped in, and after him, Paolo.

"Get your purse," Tanner ordered. "It's beer o'clock on the dock. Come drown your sorrows with the rest of us. Resistance is useless."

Paolo, looking concerned, put his arm around my shoulders. "Too soon for the blues," he murmured, "Time enough for those later. If necessary."

So off we went to the dock, rejoining the group that was arguing happily about the faults of ballroom dancing as a competitive endeavor and the virtues of ballroom dancing as demonstrated by old Fred and Ginger movies. As the three of us arrived, they paused to demand an explanation. As a distraction, I introduced Tanner.

"My apologies for Mimi's tardiness!" Tanner said brightly, "She was just getting me up to speed on the new job."

Paolo and I both smiled in admiration of Tanner's harmless, helpful, bald-faced lie. We pulled up some chairs, ordered beers, studied the menu. Soon Tanner was the focus of attention. No surprise there.

"I used to take tango lessons," Tanner was saying. "I took them for a couple of years. There is a group outside of Boston that is quite nice, actually. A bit of a drive but worth it."

"And why did you stop?" Cheryl was clearly charmed by Tanner and had already insisted at least twice that he come to the weekly lesson.

"Oh, it was a personal thing. I got involved with one of the dancers, and—" Tanner suddenly realized that he was on dangerous ground here. Maybe they wouldn't care that he was gay. Maybe I wouldn't burst into tears at the next part of the story. But he couldn't be sure. "Well, I just needed to take a break. I should give it another go, don't you think?"

"Yes!" Don said enthusiastically. "You could take Mimi when you get back to Boston. Then she would have a regular dance partner. It would be perfect."

"That would be fun," I agreed, thinking that the prospect of becoming Tanner's regular tango partner was blessedly unlikely, appallingly appropriate in several ways, and frightening on so many levels. I could see one version of my future stretching out before me, and desperately wished for a few other versions from which to choose. I glanced at Paolo, who was studying his shoes.

Tanner changed the subject by describing his efforts to learn to dance.

"And when it was my turn to be the follower, the leader couldn't see over my shoulder. And since I don't have eyes in the back of my head, we just kept crashing into other dancers until it was time to switch off. So here I am, this big person with big feet, knocking aside dancers like so many bowling pins. Strike!"

I suspected that this probably happened frequently at same-sex tango lessons. In spite of my dreary self, the

thought of Tanner crashing into people made me giggle.
This pleased him, and he carried on with his story.

"First of all, the follower really should be wearing
some heels. Of course, if I had done that, the leader
would have been looking at my belt buckle. And it's so
hard to find anything my size!" Tanner winked. The
group laughed, unaware of the very real possibility that
Tanner might choose to wear high heels in public. By the
end of the evening, Tanner had scored a dinner invitation
from Cheryl, who also invited Paolo and me. He even
arranged an actual date with Eve, one of the younger
women in the group. I was sure they would have a good
time and that Eve would have a very safe night out. And
so the evening passed.

I declined Paolo's invitation to spend the night. It
was all becoming too much, and I needed a break. Also,
the decision to put two beers and some deep fried
mushrooms on top of a quart of milk and a dozen
chocolate cookies was ill-considered, to say the least. I
didn't have to lie about my general queasiness. I promised
to show up for my tango lesson the next evening.
Although I was gratified to see a shadow of
disappointment cross Paolo's face, his sweet kiss
goodnight kept me awake and worried for hours.

"As a matter of fact, she called last night." No sooner had
I gotten tucked up for the night than the phone buzzed
with the unmistakable lilt of Ljudmila Dineva's voice on
the other end. I was just waiting for Tanner to bring her
up, as he did without fail whenever conversation was in
danger of faltering. "Tell me, Tanner, what do you think
of Schaeffer's taste in women?"

Tanner's face assumed a prissy look as he studied his

shrimp. We were having lunch with Carlos at the Bronze Gator Bar and Grill on the Peace River. "Well, I've never attempted to put those thoughts into words," he replied.

"Liar," I said simply. Tanner smiled.

"Let's just say his tastes are predictable."

"No kidding," I agreed. "The minute she walked in the door I knew he was a goner. Great body, check. Dark eyes and hair, check. Sexy clothes, check. Makeup and high heels, check, check. He never had a chance."

"I remember hoping she was nice," Tanner added.

"Who are you talking about?" Carlos had met neither of them. Tanner attempted to explain. He went over the whole story: Kannapolis, the blue fur, the presentation at the office, the tight jeans, Schaeffer, Ben, and the sister. Carlos stared in amazement. Staff at the citrus plant is uniformly male, nearly all married, hasn't changed in years and offers almost no entertainment value. And of course they don't employ anyone even remotely like Tanner.

"Ah, but you are leaving out some important aspects of the story," I pointed out. It's a rare day when I'm ahead of Tanner on the gossip curve, but I was sure today was one of those. Tanner looked at me, realizing I was holding out. He crossed his arms impatiently, raised his eyebrows, and gave me that "Out with it, little sister" look that I enjoy so much. He took a sip of his drink.

"Schaeffer and Lu are engaged. Wedding soon. I'm invited. I think you might be my date. Will you?" And I batted my eyelashes as best I could. I had practiced all morning at the computer.

When it comes to announcements of this sort, timing is everything. Tanner was in the middle of swallowing fizzy tonic water. That is very, very good timing. Choking and spitting into his napkin, he doubled over with laughter.

"You see," pointed out Carlos, "The man knew the woman was right on the first date. And the woman knew the man was right." He smiled kindly at me.

"Oh my God!" Tanner burst into laughter again, and smiled at Carlos—the kind of smile you give a well-meaning idiot, or friendly space alien. He patted Carlos on the shoulder, as if consoling a small child. Carlos looked vaguely alarmed.

"Oh, and by the way," I added, "Tammy and Steve are engaged. Wedding in June, surprise! I'm a bridesmaid. I might need a date for that one, too. I do hope your calendar is free."

I guess my edge was showing. Tanner looked at me seriously this time.

"So all of a sudden I'm the escort of choice? Not a good sign," he said quietly.

Carlos shifted uncomfortably. He cleared his throat. "Remember, Mimi, what I said. What is it that *you* need, that *you* want?"

I didn't answer. Jerome the alligator swam through my head. Brazil, I thought.

"We're renting a place up in Vermont, with a terrace overlooking a river. It's going to be spectacular, Mimi. Steve's brother is best man and you and my two sisters are the bridesmaids. I'm cruising the web for your dress right this minute!"

"What about yours?" I could see that preparations for this event were going to be the sole topic of conversation for the next seven months. Well, it's a distraction in any case, and I might need one. Tammy gave me an up-to-date account of every dress she had considered thus far.

"I'll send you the web site that has the best dresses for bridesmaids. You can see what you think. How do you feel about blue?"

"I feel fine about blue. Look, I have to go soon. I have a tango lesson."

"Ah, the hot tango teacher! I wish you the best. Do you see each other every day?"

"Well," I hadn't really thought of it that way, "I guess so. I suppose I'm just making the best of it. I come home Saturday, you know?" I could feel myself getting a bit shaky.

"So what? You know how to get on an airplane. You can visit him, or he can visit you."

"That's never going to work in the long run. And you know it."

"The long run?" Tammy had caught me in my own trap. She knew perfectly well that I had never once used this phrase in her presence about any boyfriend. I could almost see her antennae wiggling around, tasting the silence for signs of love, fear, and misery. "Maybe," she continued cautiously, "it's too early to worry about the long run? Maybe the middle run? Or just the next few months?"

"Okay," I said, trying to change the subject, "why don't you send the link for those dresses, and I'll look at it when I get back to the hotel tonight."

"I sincerely hope you are not back tonight!" Tammy was not that easily distracted. "You obviously really like this guy, and now you seem to be getting cold feet. Why?"

"Tammy, I'm not going to be on the airplane every weekend. I'm not giving up my job. I'm not moving to Florida, not that anyone has asked me to! And he does not like Boston, so that's out. I just know the situation now, that's all."

"No, you don't. You think you do, but you don't. Nothing is ever that cut and dried. Nothing is that simple, Miss Engineer. You probably have more options than you can imagine. And won't ever imagine, if you slam doors shut that quickly. Has he been unpleasant to you in any way?"

"No!" Now I was on the defensive. "Not at all."

"Then do him the courtesy of giving him a little chance. You have this picture in your head of how it all has to end up, but that is only a picture in your head. You don't even know what picture he has in his head, let alone what might actually happen."

"Yes, ma'am." She was right, of course.

"So go take a dance lesson," Tammy continued, "and don't go back to your hotel room until he tells you to do so."

"What? You're supposed to tell me to relax, go with it, be aware of what I want! That's what you usually say."

Tammy laughed. "I thought I'd just help you out by

pointing out what you want, even if you don't know it."

I knocked on the door of the dance studio. Silently, Paolo answered it, took my hand, and led me inside. He put some music on, a very smooth, lilting piece with an accordion line that flowed like melted butter. It was a bit loud, but that didn't matter, as he gave me no instructions. We just danced.

In my few days of tango experience I had only learned two or three simple patterns. We did these, over and over, in a random sequence. We did some other patterns also; I couldn't say what they were, or if they even had names. When I was little I used to dance with my father by standing on his toes and following as he moved his feet. It had seemed easy. And now, again, it was easy.

The music ended. I thought Paolo would kiss me, but instead he just put on another tune. This one had a pronounced drum, like a heartbeat, and a violin that wept. We continued as before. I became more aware of our bodies. His right hand, holding me very close, very tight. His left hand, touching my hand gently, with the softest possible touch. I danced with my eyes closed.

Another piece, this one faster, with jazzy chords and a sad swing to it. It was rich and textural. We moved faster, with smaller steps. I relaxed, letting my body be steered and placed by Paolo. Each chord was exquisitely complicated, as confusing as life itself.

We only danced. We said nothing, just danced, for two hours straight. When the last piece ended, and Paolo did not release me to go put on more music, I looked up at him. Our eyes met for the first time that evening. Then, and only then, did he kiss me, very softly, on the forehead. "May I take you to dinner?"

"Yes, please," I replied.

Tanner and I were at matching computers, checking that the up-to-date control system had been backed up properly on the spare computer. All seemed to have gone well. It looked like the job was indeed finished. Almost all the centrifuge lines were in use, and the unused ones were ready to go at any time. All that lacked were oranges, and they were on their way. The factory foreman entered the room, swearing happily.

Tanner and I said good-bye, shaking hands all around. As we drove back to the hotel, I had a chance to ask Tanner about his big night out with Eve.

"A fine girl," Tanner said, smiling, "with horrible taste in music, like you. But we had a nice time."

"Did you kiss her?" I loved asking Tanner nosy questions because he always gave as good as he got.

"Nooo," he chided. "That would be dishonest. But say, you didn't kiss Paolo last night, did you?" And we both laughed.

"So are you ready for Last Tango in Florida?" he teased. Tonight was the group lesson. I was expecting to enjoy it twice as much with Tanner there.

We arrived just a few minutes late to the lesson, waved hello and joined the circle of dancers as a pair. Tanner was quietly confidant, doing nothing terribly difficult but doing the easy stuff very well. We changed partners, the men moving forward. Ahead of me was

Cheryl, then Eve. Tanner would be fine. My new partner was the heavy man who gives instructions. I shut my eyes and tried not to listen to the music. The man took several erratic steps forward, a quick step to the side, and two steps backward, dragging me with him. "Not bad," he said. "You've improved."

At Paolo's request, the men once again moved forward and I was dancing, to my astonishment, with Carlos. Behind us was Anna, with her new partner. I assumed they had just arrived.

"What? You didn't tell me!" I was delighted to see them there. "Tanner knew, didn't he?"

Carlos laughed. "Tanner suggested it. In fact Tanner insisted. He said you needed more than one big brother this week."

I blushed. So that was it. They came to check out Paolo and keep tabs on me. Carlos and I danced. He tried to follow the directions but kept throwing in a little wiggly hip action, probably left over from his nights at the Cuban disco with Anna. Paolo came over to straighten us out.

"Take it a bit slower," Paolo said to Carlos, "and think about where you want her weight to be, on which foot. Place her on that foot so that when she steps, it's the free foot that will move. If you are going to lead, you have to take care of your follower." And he moved on to Anna and her partner.

And so it went. At one point I took a break, standing to one side and watching as Anna danced with the heavy man who gives instructions. He gave her a lot of instructions and she looked a bit embarrassed. Paolo noticed and went over to the couple, taking Anna in an open embrace and dancing with her for a few minutes. She looked much happier after that, and Paolo made the men move forward to new partners.

The lesson ended. Carlos, Anna, Tanner, and Eve surrounded Paolo, insisting that we all go out for a glass of wine. And so we went, taking Cheryl and Don along for good measure.

"For a long time Anna and I have talked about taking some kind of dance lessons," Carlos told Paolo. "I think we may have found something we both like tonight, thanks to Mimi."

"Probably more due to Tanner, I'm guessing," I interjected. People chuckled, but nobody denied it.

"I would be delighted if you came to my class," Paolo said cordially. "Every married couple should learn to tango. At least, that's my opinion."

"You are a very good teacher," Anna said sincerely, adding, "perhaps someday you will be famous for your teaching. Do you ever go to other cities to give lessons or workshops?"

"Ah, no," replied Paolo, "There is no need for that. Almost every big city already has some very good teachers."

"Then you see yourself teaching here always? For the next five or ten years anyway? Because that's probably how long it will take us to become really good dancers." Anna sounded so innocent, but all of my alarms went off at this point. Obviously this was a version of the "Where do you see yourself in ten years?" question that I was supposed to answer for myself. I could tell Paolo wasn't fooled in the least. He looked at her hard.

"If I decide to do something else or go somewhere else, I will find you another teacher. Don't worry," he said, smiling. Tanner and Carlos both suppressed a chuckle. Eve looked a bit confused.

"If you don't mind," I said, appalled by the direction this conversation was going, "I might just have to crawl under the table for a few minutes. Don't bother yourself about me!" And I started to lift the tablecloth and slide downward a bit.

"Now, Mimi," chided Tanner, "You are overreacting." He turned to Eve. "I leave for Boston tomorrow," he explained, "and Mimi leaves on Saturday. Since she has become quite fond of Paolo, her nosy friends are attempting to ask a lot of nosy questions. And we are not too subtle either. Paolo, being a sensible fellow, is not going to answer any of our questions. So instead, how about if we order a bottle of wine?"

Later that evening, much later, Paolo and I sat on his sofa drinking wine together. I apologized for the attempted interrogation, but he just laughed. I pointed out that I now had all of Friday off.

"Excellent!" replied Paolo, "When shall I pick you up?" Seeing the look on my face—a combination of surprise and distress, with a little pain thrown in, he caught himself before laughing again. "Just kidding," he said. "I think I'll keep you here tonight, if that is alright with you?"

CHAPTER 4

Saturday I went home.

I had a direct flight. No layovers, no delays, no opportunities for second thoughts. I got to my apartment and unpacked. Everything went directly into the washing machine except for a couple of items headed for the cleaners. I thought about taking them immediately, hoping a walk would empty my head of the endless confusing thoughts about my life, Paolo, the job, and everything else. Instead, the doorbell rang.

"Seriously," said Tammy, bustling into the room, "I've been trying to reach you for days." It was true. And I had been ignoring the calls. I was in such a mess that I knew it would be less than five minutes of conversation with Tammy before I lost it completely. In reality, she had been in my apartment for five seconds and I was already crying.

"Is it that bad?" Tammy set me down on the sofa and went into the kitchen, returning a few minutes later with a cup of tea, which she set before me. I looked at her, grateful to have a friend and miserable to be losing a lover. "Tell me about it. What did you do yesterday? What did he say about you leaving? Did he offer to come visit?"

"We walked on the beach," I sniffed, "and we made lunch and danced in the afternoon." It really had been a lovely day, and I know not all days can be like that one.

"Did you go out to dinner?" Tammy was handing me a wet washcloth to wipe my eyes.

"We had dinner on a little boat that cruises the canal when all the Christmas lights are up. It was lovely."

"How romantic!" Tammy smiled, trying to adjust my attitude.

"And we saw Jerome," I added, explaining, "the alligator that lives in everybody's backyard." Tammy looked confused. "He reminds me of Brazil," I added pointlessly. "and we didn't take Tanner with us."

"And what about after?" Tammy was pushing it, but I answered anyway.

"He took me to the hotel early this morning. I packed and he gave me a ride to the airport. Tanner took the car back."

"Well, what did he say when he dropped you off?" This was harder to answer. Paolo had certainly said something, but not in English. It had sounded very warm and sweet, but I had no idea what it meant. I tried to change the subject.

"I need to go do laundry."

"No you don't. You need to help me choose a

wedding dress. I have an appointment at the shop in Boston but I need backup. Not my mother, not my sisters. I need you."

I don't know how true that was. But it felt like a promising distraction. Especially when she added, "and Tanner is coming too." All of a sudden, I was home.

The dress shop was in a well-to-do neighborhood of Boston, located discretely in an old three-story building in an otherwise residential area. The three of us were greeted at the door by a thirty-something woman and escorted to a room devoted entirely to Tammy's dress purchase. The woman, Nina, found some chairs for Tanner and me, and then brought Tammy one dress at a time. We settled in for a long afternoon.

Tanner loved the first dress. It showed a lot of skin. Tammy frowned at herself in the mirror.

"We can shorten the straps," Nina explained, "so the neckline will be a little higher and you have a bit more coverage. And you need to find better underwear for all of these dresses." Tanner snickered. Nina smiled at him sweetly. I took pictures. Never for a second did I imagine Tammy would make up her mind in one afternoon. This way she could review the dresses later.

Tammy was tireless. Dresses with low cut backs, dresses with huge balloon skirts, dresses with and without lace, sheer sleeves, colored trim.

"You have no idea what you want," I complained.

"I applaud your thoroughness," countered Tanner.

"I know that seems too long," instructed Nina,

cinching up the back of a white eyelet dress embroidered with small ivory-colored cherries, "but remember you will be wearing heels. Bring them to your fitting and we can make it exactly the right length for you."

In the end Tammy narrowed it down to three choices. One was a sort of virginal Scarlett O'Hara number with untold yards of netting to keep it in place. One had more of a Ginger Rogers feel to it and could almost have been a tango dress except for the annoying sound the fabric made when it moved. The third was very straight and formal, made entirely of lace. If nuns made their habits out of doilies, they would look like this dress. In spite of their differences, they had one thing in common: Tammy looked spectacular in each of them. Tanner and I tried to do our job.

"That one has a nice neckline," I offered, "but you will be seven times as wide as the groom. Does that matter?"

"It's classic," added Nina.

"I can rent a U-Haul to get you to the church," Tanner offered.

Tammy laughed and stepped behind a curtain to change into the next one. It looked great on her. It looked like a tango dress, except quite a bit more modest. But it had that flow to it, and I said so.

"I think it shows some lumpiness," Tammy protested.

"You need to get the right underwear for all of these," Nina reminded her, "and that will fix any issues. This is a very popular dress, and we do several versions of it. Shall I get the others?"

"Let's go underwear shopping!" Tanner grinned broadly. Tammy ran off to try on the third dress.

"Too boxy!" exclaimed Tanner at the long column of lace. Tammy struck various poses. She was getting tired and a little loopy.

"Well, it doesn't show your alleged lumps," I offered.

"Or your hips or anything else," Tanner smirked, "In fact it has lumps of its own."

"Okay, Okay!" Tammy went back behind the curtain and came out a second time in dress number two. Nina fetched alternative versions. One had beading at the wrists and neckline. One had colored ribbon woven into the trim. One dress in an exceptionally small size, Nina explained, was designed for a customer who requested a trim made of blue fur.

"Oh my god," Tanner looked at me. Nina looked at him strangely. "It must be," he continued, "how could it be anybody else?"

"When," I asked Nina, "are Ljudmila and Schaeffer getting married?"

"Ah!" she exclaimed, smiling. "You know them. In three weeks, I believe."

We were deep into a plate of nachos around eight in the evening, and Tammy was on her second margarita. Tanner and I listened to the blow-by-blow description of the perfect wedding, planned for June. The mother of the bride was insisting on certain formalities. The father of the bride would pay for champagne but not beer. The groom wanted to keep it small. The bride wanted lots of flowers. The sisters of the bride had not liked any of the proposed bridesmaid dresses; no surprise there. The reception would not be in a church basement. Steve, a strict vegetarian, was proposing to take over the Indian buffet for the reception. Tammy's mom considered this to be in violation of some inexplicable social norm. Steve's uncle, a minister, would perform the ceremony. The future bride and groom made guest lists and helpful parents doubled them.

"Mom added twenty of her own friends to the guest list," complained Tammy, "saying that they had known me since I was a baby and would be completely offended if they weren't invited. She went on about how they had known me longer than any of my own friends. I suggested we invite the doctor who delivered me, and all of my former schoolteachers. This just pissed her off, of course."

Tanner clucked sympathetically. "You probably need to send invitations in February at the latest. So you have two or three months to sort it out. Or rent a circus tent!"

Tammy sighed. She signaled the waiter and ordered another margarita, even though hers was just started. "This one's for you," she said, looking at me. When the drink came, she set it in front of me.

"So," she said seriously, "has he called?"

"I don't think so," I replied.

"Oh for god's sake, what is that supposed to mean?" Impatient Tanner arched his brows.

"My phone is off."

Tanner and Tammy shared a disapproving look.

Before I could respond, Tanner snatched my purse and removed the phone. He was turning it on.

"No," I whined, "I don't want to know just yet. Please let it alone."

"You have five text messages and three missed calls. Let's see."

"Hey, you can't read my messages!"

Tanner could be outrageous, but this struck me as going way too far.

"Mimi," Tanner clutched the phone out of reach, "you need guidance, little sister. Big brother is here to help." He scanned the missed calls. "Two from Tammy and one from me. Very scary information. Good thing we are here to share this with you."

Then he looked at the text messages and started to chuckle.

"Okay, one is from me and one from Tammy. We'd been trying to reach you all day, girl, until we finally gave up and dropped in. One is from Andy. He wants to know if you are back in town. One is from Paolo, which just says please call. I think you are very rude not to answer your text messages! Ah yes, and one more."

Tanner looked at me with a wolfish leer.

"Miss Ljudmila Dineva requests the honor of having you as a bridesmaid in her upcoming wedding with Mr. Schaeffer."

In spite of my personal misery, my certainty of a doomed love life, and the general exhaustion of the past few weeks, I had to laugh. The margarita also helped. The three of us giggled for the rest of the evening, and Tanner declared that work was sure to be an interesting place on Monday.

"Tanner," I said, reaching for his hand, "promise me that if you ever get married, I can be your bridesmaid?"

"Certainly," Tanner said, beaming. "Unless, of course, you would prefer to be best man!"

I didn't call Paolo until Sunday. By then I had calmed down a bit, done some laundry, and eaten an entire quart of ice cream to quell my despair.

"Mimi, please don't be miserable over me," he said gently as soon as he heard my voice. "We are not done yet. We don't have to be done, unless you want it."

"I miss you. I'm confused. I just don't see how it can work out."

"Well, I don't know what you mean by 'work out.' My love life has always been complicated. A good affair, or relationship if you prefer, takes energy."

"I can't even see a little bit ahead. Like, when would I see you again?"

"Mimi, that's the easy part. As soon as one of us gets on an airplane."

He made it sound so simple. I knew in my stomach that it would not be simple. Paolo, sensing that his point was made, changed the subject, asking about Tanner and Tammy. I brought him up to date.

"Tanner is a good guy," Paolo commented, "and

someday I hope to meet Tammy."

"Well, you could be my date for her wedding," I suggested.

"No, no," he chided, "much sooner than that!"

For an engineer, it can take me a surprisingly long time to add two plus two, but in the end I got the sum right.

"Would you consider visiting next weekend?" I asked.

"Well," he pretended to consider, "I thought you might never ask."

Andy wanted to meet for dinner, propelling my confusion level to an all-time high. I agreed, and we met at a little Thai place in my neighborhood. Small talk has never been my strong suit, but Saturday's excursion provided enough material to get me through most of dinner. By dessert I got brave enough to ask a few questions.

"So, what did you do with yourself for the last few weeks? Did you go to Murphy's? Did you get to the Irish sessions?"

"Oh yes, all of them!" Andy smiled. He's not dense. He knew what I was asking.

"Good for you."

"Mimi, look," Andy began, meeting my eyes, "I didn't go out with anybody else. Being with you is delightful. You are lovely, and I was stupid to think I'd want anybody else more than I want you."

"Oh." I was paying attention to my feelings now, as Tammy had instructed. I felt like disappearing, right then and there. I looked at Andy. He obviously thought he had said just the right thing and looked quite pleased with himself.

"And how was Florida?" he asked with a smile., "Boring as usual?"

"Um," I waffled, "well, no. I took tango lessons."

Andy chuckled again. "Tango lessons with the retired crowd? Must have been a thrill a minute."

Pay attention to your feelings. Now I felt irritated.

"Actually, only about half of the dancers were retired. Some were my age, more or less."

"Don't tell me," Andy looked at me quizzically, "that you want to take tango lessons with me. Just please don't."

"What would be so bad about that?" I could feel myself getting defensive. Let it ride, I thought.

"Well, for starters, I would probably step on your toes." He looked at me sternly. "I detest that slow, sad music, and I don't like ballroom dancing, which I was forced to do as a kid. Please promise me you won't ask me to do this."

I met his gaze.

"I promise."

I insisted that I was exhausted, which was true. I said I needed to do laundry, also true. He asked to see me later that week. I said maybe. I said I'd let him know. I said thanks for getting in touch. I said a lot of vaguely conciliatory things. He kissed me, on the cheek. I made more excuses and went home, to Andy's obvious disappointment. Then I called Tammy to meet me for a glass of wine.

"Why am I so unexcited about this perfectly nice man?" I couldn't help but compare the ease of talking with Tammy to the awkwardness of dinner with Andy. "He's sweet. He wants to be with me. He's available, and lives in my city. What is wrong with me?"

Tammy sighed, smiling. "If there's no spark, you can't force it to happen. You two have been going out for a while. By now you should know if he is right for you or not."

"I'm supposed to know that on the first date," I replied, quoting Carlos.

"So tell me about the first date. I seem to remember you were pretty excited about it."

That was true. Tammy and I had gone to hear the Irish session, and I flirted with a cute young man with dark eyes and a quiet charm. I saw him flirt with a few other women that night also, which was reassuring. My previous boyfriend was in the habit of flirting with guys, and I appreciated the solid evidence of heterosexual preferences. When he asked me to meet him for dinner the next day, I was elated.

"Well, you were there when he asked me out. I thought I'd won the lottery."

"That was before the first date," countered Tammy. "What about the date itself?"

I laughed. "It was kind of a disaster," I confessed.

"What!" Tammy pretended to be indignant. "You never told me about that!"

"I don't tell you everything," I said, "especially when it makes me look kind of bad."

"Do go on," she ordered.

For our first date, Andy had taken me to a concert. Maybe he wanted to show that he had unusual taste in music, or maybe he was being cheap. It was a house concert—somebody had arranged for a musician to play folk music in their living room. They set up chairs and advertised by word of mouth. Andy knew everybody in the room, which made it impossible to flirt effectively. We didn't even hold hands for most of the evening.

"I'd say that's a weak start," Tammy snorted at my story.

"Ah, but it doesn't end there." The musician was a huge woman with a decent but not very interesting voice, mediocre guitar skills, and an amazing memory for lyrics. Every song had at least seven verses, and seven more choruses between them. These were long songs about ships sinking at sea, lobstermen, and lumberjacks. She sang at least four songs about lumberjacks.

"Who knew there were that many songs about lumberjacks?" Tammy asked, pensively.

"And we were all supposed to sing along on the choruses," I said and grinned. Tammy is one of the few people who knows how I sing. Not well at all, as it turns out.

"Andy has a beautiful voice." It was true. He sang along without hesitation, adding a lovely bass harmony to the choruses.

"Did you sing?" Tammy is so nosy.

"I tried." The memory of this still embarrasses me. I squeaked on the high notes and choked on the low notes. The middle notes were not exactly on pitch either. People on either side of me turned to look for the source of the unwanted jazz chords. "Andy was very polite about it, and actually quite encouraging," I added.

"What about after the concert?"

"Well, we hung around really late because he knew everybody. I couldn't leave because he was my ride. By the time he dropped me off, we were both exhausted."

"So, did you make out at least a little?" Tammy was completely relentless.

"Um, no," I admitted, "but it was okay with me. I had work the next day."

Tammy looked confused.

"Why did you go out with him a second time? It sounds perfectly awful."

I thought about this. I wasn't sure.

"Memory is a slippery thing. I don't remember thinking it through. I think I just wanted to give it another chance. I was hopeful. It's good to be hopeful, right?"

"And so you went out with him for five months. And at the end of five months, were you still just giving it another chance?" I thought about this description of our dates. All in all, it was a pretty good picture of how the entire business had gone. Andy would take me somewhere I didn't particularly like, and then we'd go back week after week. I would suggest something else, and it would be a struggle to get him to try it. He seemed to want good company, but not romance.

"Well, yeah," I conceded, "I guess you are right. He's just such a decent guy, I feel guilty for not wanting him more. And I guess he is attracted to me more than I thought, because he didn't go out with anybody else while I was away."

"Just because he didn't go out with other people, does not mean that you have to continue dating him." Tammy was firm on this one. "Unless, of course, you want to. What do you want, Mimi?"

I couldn't say for sure. But it was becoming clearer that Andy, whatever his virtues, would not be my lover again.

The first Monday back after any job on site is filled with paperwork. Daily notes on work done, lists of expenses, receipts attached, alcohol subtracted; all of these must be post-processed into a spreadsheet. I had my office door shut for a few hours. By the time it was done Jeff the accountant had gone to lunch. I headed out to do the same, but was captured in the parking lot by Lu.

"Mimi, you're back!" she said cheerfully. "Did you get my text message?"

I allowed that I had, adding, "Of course, I'm honored to be part of your wedding party, Lu. Just let me know what you need me to do."

Ljudmila Dineva smiled fetchingly and insisted on taking me to lunch. Over salad and iced tea I got to hear every detail of the upcoming nuptials. Three bridesmaids, no less, would grace the altar: me, Lu's sister Tsvetanka, and a Bulgarian cousin. Grozda, the cousin, was arriving just for the occasion and spoke, according to Lu, very little English. Schaeffer was the very picture of restraint with only his two brothers as groomsmen.

"Mimi, I wanted so badly for you to be part of this. I feel you have been so supportive and helpful: a mentor, really. Some people in the office are just so judgmental. Ben really dislikes me and I don't think he is the only one. Dan is good. He understands. He said I could have two days off before the wedding and the whole week afterward for a honeymoon. We'll miss the money but I think a honeymoon is important, don't you? It gets things off on the right foot."

I smiled. I wouldn't know. But it was good to see Ljudmila happy and marginally less paranoid than usual.

Lu went over the invitation list. About a quarter of the people at work were invited. Schaeffer had his large family and his college friends on the list. Lu had her sister, her cousin, and her grandmother. She explained that all of her relatives in Bulgaria had chipped in to pay for the cousin's visa and air ticket. I asked how long the visa allowed her to be in the country.

"As long as she's in school," Lu replied. After some prodding, she explained further, "I enrolled her at the community college and paid one semester's tuition. They arranged the paperwork for the visa. She is my favorite little cousin! I can't leave her in Bulgaria. There's no work for her there and she would have to clean houses. Schaeffer says she is welcome to live with us. We are going to buy a house big enough for us, and my cousin, and my grandmother. We are house hunting now! It's so exciting."

I thought of the one time Schaeffer and I had gone out to lunch together. It was a slow day and almost everybody else was away at some factory or another. When the bill came, Schaeffer calculated what each of us owed down to the last penny. He computed the tip in proportion to the cost of our lunches. Mine came to exactly ten cents more than his. I put in an extra quarter and he actually made change. Schaeffer had never impressed me as an overly generous person. He was fair, yes, but not terribly generous. He must, I concluded, be completely smitten. Or insane. Possibly dusted with fairy dust. Granny and the cousin are going to move in with the newlyweds. Oh, my!

"I really hope you are going somewhere spectacular for your honeymoon," I said, thinking that it might be the last bit of privacy they would have for some time.

"Well, it's almost December and we're trying to save up for the house, so we're keeping it simple and just going to the Keys for a week. I think it will be lovely."

Ljudmila stood up and pulled her cashmere hoodie over her head. Several gold necklaces got caught in the weave and she extracted them. Her long fingernails were the color of a Halloween pumpkin, with silver tips. They contrasted smartly with the deep blue of the sweater. I threw my denim jacket over my boring white shirt. We walked back to the office and I broached the inevitable question.

"So Lu," I ventured, "for your wedding, what do you want me to wear?"

"I'm not much good until the second cup of coffee goes down," I offered lamely.

Paolo was in good spirits and perused the weekend newspaper looking for adventures. I wondered what he might find in Boston to keep us occupied for the afternoon or evening. It is funny how having a guest makes you aware of how routine your life is. I always found stuff to do, but it tended to be the same stuff week after week. Maybe I'm more like Andy than I care to admit.

"Oh, wow," he said. "Look. They have a jellyfish exhibit at the museum of science. Do you like jellyfish? They are so graceful."

"Sure," I was relieved not to have to make a decision. It would be fun to hang out with Paolo no matter what we decided to do. He looked at me sideways.

"You don't sound too excited," he observed. "I'm trying to find something we'd both like to do."

"Well, you are the guest," I said, smiling, "and I should be finding things you like to do. And I'm doing a terrible job. Maybe if I finish this cup of coffee?"

Paolo had arrived Thursday evening. I warned him that I had to work the next day. When I got home on Friday, the apartment had been straightened up and dinner was bought and prepared. There were flowers on the table. By my calculation, Saturday should be payback time and that meant I should find something outstanding for us to do.

"Jellyfish are okay with me," I said. "And there is a great Chinese restaurant near the aquarium. Do you like Chinese food?" I asked.

"Yes, and you can't get any good Asian food in Port Charlotte," he replied. "I like this plan."

"And there is a milonga tonight in Somerville," I added, "if you're not tired of tango."

"Never!" smiled Paolo.

So off we went to see jellyfish. Tank after tank displayed circling jellies, some translucent blue, some with iridescent sparkles, some milky white moons trailing comet tails. The jellies pulsed rhythmically, pumping themselves through the backlit waters. Paolo and I held hands tightly. It was strangely romantic.

At lunch we had the opportunity to order jellyfish, which we took. Also sea cucumber, pressed duck, and an appetizer wrapped in leaves. Paolo tucked in happily.

"Dancers aren't supposed to overeat," he said guiltily, "but I haven't had real Chinese food since I moved to Florida. Boston certainly does have its attractions!" He winked at me.

"Excellent!" I laughed. "But here is a question. The milonga doesn't start until nine o'clock. It's only one thirty. What shall we do with the afternoon?"

"Oh, I don't know. We could buy you another dress!"

I wasn't quite sure how to respond. I actually needed another dress. Ljudmila said I could wear any dress I liked as long as it was a solid color in the peach/apricot/salmon family. She made this request sound easy, but I had little idea where to begin a search for such a dress, and I only had two weeks. Slightly embarrassed, I explained the situation to Paolo.

"Oh, that's easy!" he replied, "Give me your phone!"

Without thinking it through, I did so. He pulled up my contacts and made a call. I should have known. At the other end of the line I heard Tanner, howling. After a few minutes Paolo hung up.

"He says to meet him at Copley Place. This is sure to be as amusing as our shopping excursion in Port Charlotte." I laughed at Paolo's enthusiasm.

"Okay, but Boston is a lot bigger and Tanner is tireless. Are you sure you are up for it?"

"Ha!" said Paolo. "The question is, are you?"

I sighed. "It doesn't matter. It has to get done one way or the other. And I need all the help I can get. And I would never have asked Tanner!" I laughed again. "Well, I hope you are both entertained."

We waited outside the subway station at Copley Place. Paolo was about to phone Tanner when we heard someone whistling. I turned to see Tanner, who broke out in song, with considerable attitude and recognizable pitch. I didn't recognize the tune. Tanner gave up and patted me on the shoulder. "Remember that old movie, *Bridesmaids*?" he said. "That was me, covering Britney Spears."

"It's great to see you!" Paolo seemed genuinely to appreciate Tanner's offbeat approach to life. Paolo was one of the few sweethearts I had ever let near Tanner, due to the unpredictable nature of the consequences.

Paolo explained the details of the afternoon quest.

"So the theme of the wedding is Fifty Shades of Apricot?" Paolo and I giggled as Tanner went on. "Ljudmila knows exactly what she is doing. One woman in a hundred is going to look good in head to toe solid peach. Or apricot. Or salmon. But we," he said, his arm encompassing the three of us, "are brilliant. And we will find a way to work it."

"I am counting on you," I replied, completely honestly.

"First of all, we must extend the boundaries of our search. She said 'solid color.' Well, she didn't mean that. She just meant no prints. We can allow ourselves a little trim, some contrasting details. You know, to break up the sea of salmon, which are overfished anyway. And we can tone it down. It can be a muted salmon, which is easy because they don't talk much in the first place: apricots and peaches likewise. If we get a natural fiber we can over-dye it to get exactly the right effect. Mimi, what's your best color?"

"Black?" I offered. Tanner's expression indicated that he thought I was being difficult.

"Well, I wear a lot of it," I said, apologetically.

Tanner and Paolo hit the formal dress section of store after store, fanning out, coming back together, consulting and setting off again, like hounds after a rabbit. The rabbit turned out to be elusive. The worst dresses were in special sections reserved for bridesmaids and mothers of brides. After awhile we didn't even bother with those. Who knew that blue could look that bad?

"Too puffy!" I tried on a pale peach item with way too much skirt and puffed sleeves as big as grapefruits.

"You would definitely get your money's worth of fabric," Tanner pointed out.

"Maybe I should just get a pattern and fabric and make it myself."

"No," said Paolo and Tanner simultaneously.

The next dress was several sheer layers of pink silk. Tanner held it up to me, and argued that it could be dyed the right color if I liked it. Paolo claimed I could tango in it. Or wear it later, to Tammy's wedding.

"Only if it got dyed again after Lu's wedding," I pointed out, "because Tammy wants blue. Turquoise blue, to be exact." But in the end, the fit was just exactly wrong.

We hit eight stores in three hours. Racing through the racks, they managed to make me try on a total of six dresses. Two were indescribably ill fitting, two were just plain ugly, and two were definitely not in the right fish/fruit color family.

"But do you like any of them?' Paolo crossed his arms.

"Well, one was okay and one was actually good, but neither of those were salmon. Or peach, or apricot, or tangerine. My favorite was the forties number with the full skirt, but what a horrible shade of pink."

"American in Paris," offered Paolo. "It could work. It's silk and can be dyed."

"The melon queen of North Dakota," Tanner countered. "No way. She has to look at least as good as the bride."

"Oh, come on! I weigh thirty pounds more than the bride, my hair is mouse colored, and I look like the geek I am. Can we set a reasonable standard here?" I always worry when Tanner sets the standards. The man can obsess.

"It's a delicious thirty pounds," Paolo defended me against myself. "Would you rather have one scoop of ice cream or three?"

"How about one. Right now." And so we paused to consider our options over some soft serve.

"I know a place," Tanner said thoughtfully, "but you

might find it a little odd. "

"Sure," I said, "We've tried a lot of stuff, why not one more?" And so off we went, first by subway to the edge of Boston and then on foot to a college neighborhood that I knew was not too far from Tanner's apartment. He led us to a small shop on a trendy little street. There were large hats in the window with feathers sweeping out of them, and some vintage items on hangers covered in stuffed pink silk.

"Tanner!" cried the salesman as we entered. "My favorite ex! What wonderful excuse brings you to my little heaven?"

"Paolo, Mimi, this is my friend Todd," Tanner started to explain.

"Friend, indeed," agreed Todd, "and much more than that at one point! And now I never see Tanner and I'm so sad." Todd made a sad face and then brightened up. "Ahem," he continued, "how may I help you?"

Tanner explained the entire situation, including Ljudmila's descent on our little company, my romance with Paolo, and the difficult job of finding the perfect dress in the right fruity, fishy color.

"Oh my, that's a tall order," Todd looked me up and down. "But no worry, you are in the hands of a professional now."

"And it would be good if she could use it to tango later," Tanner added.

"Fabulous!" agreed Todd, adding, "I do so love to tango. Do you remember our evenings at dance class dear?" Todd batted his eyes at Tanner.

"They were a delight, darling."

I could see that Paolo was mightily amused. Todd took us upstairs to a room full of dresses, some old, some new, each one unique. He pulled out an off-white lace dress that looked far too big. He insisted I try it on. I came out wearing a loose tent gathered at the bust.

"Now, look," he said, gathering the dress from behind me. "I'm guessing that one thing you have that your Bulgarian friend does not have is boobs. Nice ones. So this is where we will give you the advantage." He pulled the front of the dress down to show cleavage. Then he tightened the back of it, not just at the bust but, with his other hand, all the way down. He marched me to the mirror. "I can alter it so it fits you like this. Do you like the fit?"

"Can you make it flare out at the bottom so she can dance?" asked Tanner, cocking his head to one side.

"It isn't melon or peach or apricot or salmon," I pointed out.

"I can make it flare at the bottom. Of course I can," Todd sighed, "and I can dye it a fabulous color. That is perfect on you. That you will love."

Paolo, who had been quiet until now, offered his opinion. "Trust him."

Todd looked at Paolo with interest. "Thank you. I thank you. Rhode Island School of Design thanks you. I plan to make her look so good that you and Tanner fight over who gets to tango with her. Are you going to the wedding too?"

Paolo looked at me. "Only if I'm invited."

"Really?" I found myself tearing up a bit. "Of course I want you to come with me. You don't mind coming back?"

"Oh, for god's sake, Mimi," Tanner snorted, "the man is in love. Of course he wants to come back. And steal my date."

"Sorry!" smiled Paolo, "but I'm a desperate man as you can see."

"Well!" exclaimed Tanner. And after only the slightest pause, "Todd, will you be my date to a very special wedding in two weeks?"

Todd blushed prettily. "It would be my greatest pleasure."

I should have realized that Paolo would know dancers at the milonga. He used to live in the Boston area, and as soon as we walked into the room, quite a few people gathered around to say hello. Most of them were women. He had to promise them all a dance just to get in the door and find a table.

We danced two dances before one woman tapped him. He excused himself for two dances with her, turning down another invitation to come back to the table and take my hand for two more. And so the evening went, two on and two off, until Paolo began to refuse their offers. All of these women seemed to know Paolo, and they were all very good dancers, at least as far as I could tell.

I found myself becoming jealous. He looked so good with them. They pressed against him in close embrace. A close embrace in tango is like nothing else. It makes certain steps more difficult, because you are so close together that it is easy to tangle up the feet. The woman pushes upward toward the man, her legs like springs. Never leaning—no—but still with a firm contact. The man, if he chooses, can drop his arms and lead only with his chest, his weight. It is incredibly sexy to watch, and even sexier to do. These ladies were experienced dancers and added their own flair to the moves. I could hardly stand it.

I had to wonder why the scene bothered me. I never felt this way with the group in Port Charlotte. I got to dance less with Paolo at those milongas, but I never felt jealous or like my beginner's efforts were somehow inappropriate. Here I felt slightly embarrassed for no reason that I could pin down. I sipped a glass of wine and wondered.

I distracted myself from my own emotions by watching Tanner and Todd. They also danced in close embrace. I found it hot, even hotter than the mixed couples. They often switched leads. Only they could have said who was the leader and who the follower. When Paolo left me to dance with someone else, occasionally one of them would take over for him. Both were quite good, and I felt strangely at ease pressed up against them. After Paolo had danced with all of his old friends, he gave them no chance at a second dance. Instead, he took Tanner, then Todd, then me in succession, with the remaining two left to dance together. At the end, we all went out for a glass of wine.

"Mimi, you are an excellent dancer!" Tanner seemed genuinely surprised.

"I wouldn't go that far, but thank you. And thank you both for dancing with me."

"That was fun," Paolo said, looking at me sideways. "Did you have fun, Mimi?"

"Well,"— I didn't want to explain the wash of feelings I had watching Paolo dance with other, wonderfully graceful, women—"yes. I enjoyed dancing with all three of you. I have to say, though, something about the atmosphere was not quite as nice as the milonga in Port Charlotte. I can't explain it. How come you know so many people?"

Paolo smiled. "I used to live here. I learned to dance my first tango here. I went to every milonga there was to practice, practice, practice. I've danced with most of these ladies many, many times. And I haven't been back for six years, except for a couple of trips to take workshops from some very special teachers."

"Everybody wanted to dance with you," Todd teased Paolo.

"Yes," agreed Tanner, "and nobody wanted to dance with us. I suppose we should have gotten out there and asked people. But I thought at least one or two of the men would have taken pity on Mimi when the women whisked you away."

"Ah, but I was surrounded by three handsome men," I pointed out, "and they were probably intimidated."

"No," sighed Paolo, "that's just Boston. The dancers are much too serious. It must be hard to take yourself that seriously. But you are right, Mimi, the dance scene is a little intense and can verge on competitive. It's one of the many reasons I left. Often the very best dancers forget the first rule of dancing."

"And what is that?" Todd asked.

"Make sure that your partner is having fun," Paolo replied, "because giving pleasure to the other person is the very point of the dance."

"And of so many other parts of life as well," mused Tanner.

"I don't mean that he wasn't nice," Tammy explained. "Of course he seems quite sweet. He just wasn't how I imagined, that's all." I had made sure Tammy had a chance to meet Paolo over breakfast on Sunday morning.

I pressed her: "What exactly do you mean?"

"Well, you made it sound like he was incredibly handsome. He's attractive, of course, but the way you fell for him, I thought he was this hunk."

"I think he's handsome!"

"Of course you do. You are in love. I guess he's just not my type, not that he has to be anybody's type but yours. He's so thin and his face is so angular. It's a sort of Latin look, but still I imagined him differently. And you never showed me any pictures either!" Tammy chided. "So of course I was bound to be surprised. But I liked him. When is he coming back?"

"In a week and a half, to be my date at Ljudmila's wedding. He will spend the weekend, of course." I giggled. "Tanner is determined that Paolo and I will be the hottest couple at the event. He is adamant that we will tango spectacularly. I think he just wants to annoy Lu. But he is dragging me to every tango lesson and milonga he can find, to practice."

"Tanner is your big tango date?"

"Three times this week already."

"And you dance all the dances with him? Tanner knows how to dance?"

"I dance every third dance with Tanner. Then I dance one with Todd, then I sit one out." I had to explain about Todd. By the end of my description of our double date at the milonga, Tammy was rolling. I had to admit that, in spite of how distracting Lu and Schaeffer were at work, they were not my main entertainment at this moment. It was the daily update from Tanner that I anticipated with joy. His newly rekindled relationship with Todd was occupying all his spare time and energy, and he seemed to be enjoying it tremendously. I wondered why they had broken up in the first place. And our tango trio was a source of endless fun. I could only guess what the other dancers thought about us, but every possible guess made me laugh. I couldn't wait to see Lu's face at the reception, with the four of us trading partners. I sincerely hoped her granny wouldn't get upset. And Tanner, who kept his orientation fairly private at work, was completely overjoyed at the prospect of letting it show at the wedding.

"What if they don't play any tango music at the reception?"

"Oh, you can tango to anything slow to medium fast," I said, adding, "if you have a good leader."

"What should I do?" Ben seemed truly distraught. He had stopped by my office, stepped in, and closed the door quietly but firmly. He was almost whispering because, in our building, the walls are made of some cheap stuff that resembles a plastic container. Sound goes right through.

"Schaeffer's a good friend, but you know how I feel about all of this." Ben waved his hand in the general direction of Lu's office. "Too fast, too soon. And I know Lu doesn't want me there."

I was impressed. Schaeffer had put Ben on the guest list for his wedding. I was sure that Lu didn't like it, and equally sure I'd be hearing her side of it at some point this week. I was impressed because, since he met Lu, Schaeffer had done everything to try to please her. Now that he was about to marry her, it appeared that Schaeffer's backbone was starting to show.

I knew exactly what Ben ought to do, but he wasn't going to like it.

"Just go to the wedding and enjoy yourself," I said firmly. "Enjoy Schaeffer's happiness. Be happy for Lu. She is not a bad person, Ben."

Ben grunted darkly. "I suppose not," he admitted. "But I'm not sure I approve of the way she is manipulating Schaeffer. I don't think he realizes to what extent she is running his life already, and they aren't even married yet."

"They seem to be making each other really happy. Try to focus on that. Go to their wedding and cheer for them. It's really the right thing to do."

Ben sighed. "I suppose you are right. But really, Mimi, what do you think about all of this? Lu clings to Schaeffer like she can't do anything without him. I suppose it's great for his ego. Is that what it's about?"

I've been with this firm for six years, and known Ben the entire time. This was the first time we'd ever had a conversation about the personal life of a colleague. The temptation to engage in girl gossip with Ben was strong, but I knew he would think less of me as a result.

Of course I had my opinions about what Lu and Schaeffer brought to their relationship, but they were complex opinions and didn't always flatter either one of them. I don't think I'm catty, just realistic. I'm also error prone. I'm off the mark so often on my guesses about others that the best I can do is to give each guess a probability. With fifty percent probability, Schaeffer is sucked in by the idea that he can be somebody's hero. I give a sixty-five percent probability to the idea that Lu's main motivation is U.S. citizenship for herself and as many family members as she can manage. On the other hand, maybe she just wants security, and to have a house and kids, like most other women our age. Or maybe she wants her hero, and Schaeffer has volunteered for the job. I'd say I'm ninety-five percent sure that the sex is very good between them.

Am I going to say any of this to Ben? Hell no, this is an engineering firm. Maybe after I've been here 25 years. Maybe after three margaritas. Maybe when I'm menopausal. Or possibly retired. I tried to deflect Ben's question.

"Well, everybody has an ego," I agreed, "including Schaeffer. That's always part of the picture, isn't it? And nobody can see inside a relationship, to see what really makes it tick. So I'm afraid we'll have to settle for ignorance and just wish them well."

"Maybe after they're living alone together for a while, things will calm down around here and go back to normal," Ben mused.

"Too much drama?" I smiled.

"Oh my, yes."

"Well," I grinned, "It will be a while before they live alone together. Granny and the young cousin are moving right in with them. It will be a well-supervised marriage."

Sometimes I can be really evil. I didn't need to tell Ben all of that stuff! But I certainly enjoyed doing so. His reaction was splendidly rewarding.

"Oh my god! Oh my god!" Ben looked at me and registered the smirk on my face.

"Oh my god!" We both said together, and burst out laughing loud enough that the whole office could hear us through the Tupperware walls.

Tsvetanka drew in a sharp breath and met Ljudmila's eyes.

"Is something wrong?" They all looked at me. Five hours to go until the wedding and stress levels were already way too high. A mild and seemingly innocuous discussion had escalated, rising not in volume but in pitch and speed. Ljudmila had said something, in a very big-sisterly tone of voice, which had clearly offended Tsevtanka.

"Oh no," protested Tsvetanka, "it's nothing." She turned to Lu and continued, in a low voice, a rapid-fire discussion that was returned with equal fervor. The cousin looked on with some alarm. The situation was degenerating into a Bulgarian tizzy, of which I understood nothing. I tried again.

"What seems to be the problem?" Lu looked at me and sighed.

"I have an uncle in Colorado," she said, "who was

supposed to be here. He was supposed to walk me down the aisle. Isn't that what you do here? Somebody is supposed to give you away, no? But now, at the last minute, he cannot come. Tanka wants me to have our grandmother do it, but I refuse. It doesn't look right, and Schaeffer will think it's strange. It would be strange, right?"

"That's a tough one," I agreed. "I guess it would be stranger to walk down the aisle by yourself. We could escort you of course."

Lu wrinkled her nose. I could just imagine her, watching television shows about weddings and trying to arrange a perfect one, on fairly short notice. Everybody knows that the bridesmaids are not giving the bride away. I wondered what she had said to Tsvetanka.

"Do you have any male friends at all, besides Schaeffer?" I asked. "Any of them would make the procession look fairly normal."

Lu looked dejected. Here, I thought, is where you pay for your paranoia. Inspiration suddenly hit.

"Hey Lu," I said, "Would it be fair to say that your work is sort of your new family here?"

Lu looked at me oddly. "In a way, I suppose that is true," she agreed.

"Well, who from work have you invited?"

Lu hesitated, and nervously gave the list. Not too many people from work were coming, although they had invited most of them.

"Want me to solve your problem right now?" What could she say? She was trapped. I sent Tanner a text message, and a minute later the phone rang.

"How is it going, Mimi? Are you spectacularly beautiful yet? Are you stunning?"

I laughed. Lu and Tsvetanka listened closely.

"The bride is spectacular," I replied, "and we need your help."

"At your service always!" Tanner exclaimed cheerily. "Do you need more flowers? A button sewed on? Something borrowed? Something blue?"

I explained. There was an explosion of laughter at the other end, a short side conversation with Todd, a second round of laughter.

"This may be a once in a lifetime opportunity!" I pointed out. More laughter. I had a hard time keeping a straight face, the phone pressed to my ear so nobody but me could hear. Finally I did get an answer. I turned to Lu.

"What time do you want him here, and should he wear a tux?"

Lu beamed. "A tux would be fantastic. In an hour or so we'll have a short practice. Maybe he could get here by then?" And so, more or less, he did.

You would think that nothing is easier than being a bridesmaid. All you have to do is walk down the aisle at the right time, stand in the right location, say nothing and try not to doze. But the bride is giving her stress away like sugar coated Jordan almonds, and everybody gets some. Tsvetanka almost cried before getting all the way down the aisle. The little cousin looked terrified. I walked a bit too fast and messed up the perfect spacing of the three of us. Even Tanner looked a little worried for Lu's sake as he

121

escorted her gently down the aisle, patting her arm as they walked. Lu looked gorgeous, nervous, radiant.

I guess I always knew that Schaeffer's family was a bit blue blood, waspy, upper classy. He had mentioned before that they wondered why he chose to be an engineer, rather than work in the financial sector or some other less messy occupation. Today they were lined up to see him get married. The look on his mother's face was precious. I couldn't tell if it was simple relief that their nerdy son had found a girl, or a deep fear that he had found his match, and then some. Lu was spectacular, but I'm sure she didn't resemble any of the nice girls Schaeffer's mom would have picked—no, not in the slightest. At least they had the little white church, which looked as New England as it possibly could for the occasion, with a dusting of snow and fake candles in the windows.

The ceremony was so traditional I almost did doze off. I caught Tanner looking at me menacingly a few times. I think he was just trying to keep me awake. Finally it was over. We recessed. Nobody fell down or blew their nose on their sleeve or in any other way transgressed. We were a success. And now it was time to party.

It should not have surprised me. Paolo is, after all, incredibly attractive. Even if Tammy doesn't think so, Tsvetanka certainly did. Seated between Paolo and her cousin, she talked exclusively to him, leaving me to exchange small talk and meaningful glances with Tanner and Todd at my end of the table. I was suffering a raging fit of jealousy by the time dinner ended and the dance music started. After the first waltz by the happy couple, I heard Paolo declining her offer, saying that he definitely had a partner for the next dance.

The band was covering a Grateful Dead tune. Not the perfect tango scenario. But Paolo just moved to the beat and took me with him, in close embrace. Everybody else was doing the usual bopping up and down that goes with such music, and there we were just having a great time being weird. The music ended and we returned to our seats. Passing the table where Ben and Dan sat, I caught their eye. They were actually gaping at us, jaws slack with astonishment.

I suppose Tanner's plan was working. I guess we looked pretty hot out there doing a sexy dance to a fabulously inappropriate tune. I wondered if Lu was annoyed. We returned to our table and sat one out. Lu looked at me with new eyes, and Tsvetanka was oddly quiet. The little cousin smiled at me. "Very pretty!" she said in her limited English. I thanked her. Paolo gallantly offered her his hand. Astonished, she let him lead her to the dance floor where they did some very simple steps at arm's length. I could see she was thrilled.

"I adore beginners," he confided, sitting down beside me. What a thing to say.

"I adore you," I said, automatically, realizing it was true.

Don brought the small boat about. I shivered slightly in the Florida winter, and Paolo touched my shoulder lightly.

"When will you visit again?" Cheryl smiled kindly at me. "We would love to see you next time you come."

At that moment I was contented, and it registered as a strange sensation. I am suspicious of contentment, and I associate it with boredom. I snuggled a bit closer to Paolo.

"It makes me happy to come here," I admitted.

Paolo chuckled. "Then come more often!" he admonished. It was true. He flew to Boston three times for every time I managed to get away for a long weekend in Florida. I didn't feel too guilty about this, as he had professional connections, dance friends, and other ties to the Boston area. When he visited me, he was always busy. It was reassuring to think that he had interesting stuff to do while I was at work.

"Oh, I'd love to," I said, almost truthfully, "but work eats up a lot of time."

Cheryl studied me. "How important is your work to you?" she asked. And, seeing the fierce look that I couldn't completely suppress, she added, "I mean, would you ever consider working part time? Three quarters? Half? Think of all the adventures you could have with a little more time."

"Spoken like the successfully retired!" I teased, "What if I ever want to buy a house, have a child, send it to college, be normal? Doesn't that stuff take money? And most of the time, my job is pleasant, if not actually fun. What would I do with myself all day, without some problem to solve?"

"Well," suggested Paolo, "if you aren't paid to solve problems for other people, you could solve the problems you choose to solve."

I looked at him blankly.

"That's sort of what has happened to me," he explained. "I still think about some interesting problems, but I choose what I work on and when I work on it. It's a great freedom."

"Sure," I said, "but you made a bit of money before you had that option."

"True enough," he said, smiling. "I'm just saying that finding interesting things to do is never the issue."

"I guess not," I agreed. But inside I wondered if it could ever really be so. I know how easy it is to slide into a routine that keeps you really busy but is, nonetheless, deeply boring. I thought of Andy, who is completely contented with the same job, the same music, the same thin relationships, year in and year out. I, meanwhile, was having fantasies about Brazil. To me, the reassuring routine felt like a trap. Now, of course, everything was exciting. I adored Paolo, was excited to improve my dancing, had weddings to plan for even though they weren't mine, and still had a job worth doing: keeping America in paper, ethanol, and orange juice.

"By the way," Don said, releasing me from Cheryl's uncomfortable question, "Your tango has gotten quite good. Everybody noticed it at the milonga last night. You must be putting some time into it in Boston."

I smiled. I had to explain that, in Paolo's absence, Tanner and Todd made me come along to many a lesson, and every milonga. If I was getting practice, it was largely their doing. And if I got better, well, I couldn't really tell. At the Boston lessons my partners gave me pointers constantly, especially when they stepped on my toes. And at the dances, none of them offered to tango with me. I danced with Tanner and Todd, both of whom were good leaders and considerate partners. So I couldn't have said I was getting better. It was nice to hear it from Don.

"I love the tango scene here," I added. "It's much more relaxed."

"It's true," Paolo agreed. "We have a great group here."

Don and Cheryl appeared flattered by this statement, and also slightly embarrassed.

"Of course, one reason it is more relaxed here is that there aren't two dozen women hitting on Paolo," I teased. "I get pretty jealous at those dances in Boston, if Paolo is with me."

Cheryl smiled. "You should definitely be spending more of your time here then. Such a romantically safe environment."

Paolo smiled gently. "Mimi has nothing to fear," he said reassuringly.

Cheryl laughed. "Except her own choices," she replied.

CHAPTER 5

I dropped the sheaf of papers I was carrying and looked at Dan, astonished.

"Are you serious?"

"Completely. More than sixteen tons of oranges are processed for juice in Brazil."

"You want me to go to Brazil?"

Dan looked at me as if I were a dimwitted child, which perhaps I am. "I don't see how you can help them install the upgrade any other way," he said, stating the obvious. "This is Cutrale, the biggest citrus processor in Brazil, and probably the world. They want a software upgrade. It's a foot in the door for us. A very big door."

"Why on earth would they hire us? Surely there are engineers in Brazil." I spoke rationally, but my pulse was racing. Dan looked at me as if I were a slightly intelligent child, after all.

"Good question. I've been wondering that myself.

They know we do some work at citrus plants in Florida, and are somewhat expert in this particular software."

"I don't speak Brazilian."

Dan laughed. "You don't speak Portuguese either," he corrected. "I know that. They know that. They said they would partner our engineer with theirs, and theirs speaks English fluently. Their engineer would be responsible for the installation, but ours would function as a consultant."

"That is really weird," I said. The companies we work with are usually trying to cut the budget in every possible way.

"I know," Dan agreed, "but look at it this way. They have a huge operation, running night and day. To complete the installation they will have to shut down briefly. I think the extra engineer is some kind of cheap insurance that the shutdown will be extremely short. I think, basically, that is the job. It should take about a week."

"Wow," I commented stupidly. "Amazing. Yes, of course." I felt like hugging Dan, or maybe turning cartwheels in the hall. Either of these would be unprofessional, so I picked up my folder from the floor, took the large information packet Dan handed me, and walked calmly to my office. When the door was closed I jumped up and down for a few minutes and then called Paolo.

"I could go to the factory for a week and then you could meet me there and I could take some vacation time and we could do stuff!"

Paolo was strangely quiet. Somehow I had assumed he would jump at the chance to go somewhere interesting, but instead he hesitated. Then he asked questions. Where was this place exactly? How long would the job take? What's the nearest big city? When exactly were the dates? And he wondered aloud to himself how many of his tango classes his students would have to miss. By the end of our conversation I was frustrated and disappointed. My elation at the prospect of a trip to Brazil slowly gave way to the realization that I might be going by myself.

Ah, well, I thought. My fantasies of a trip to Brazil were solo flights anyway.

Manuel, a representative of Cutrale, met me at the São Paolo airport, greeted me profusely, and drove me a few hours to a big hotel in the center of a small city. Along the way we chatted, his English close to perfect and my Portuguese limited to please and thank you. The landscape was flat and agricultural, and reminded me more of south Florida than of my fantasies about Brazil.

The town of Araraquara seems to exist because of oranges. A few hundred kilometers inland from São Paolo, a city of over ten million, little Araraquara has only two hundred thousand residents; it's like a little island afloat in a sea of orange groves. Entering the town, we passed through neighborhoods of small, low houses, fortified by cement walls and locked gates. The center of town had some larger buildings, one of which was my very clean and modern hotel.

"You must be very tired," Manuel observed. "Get some rest and I will pick you up for dinner."

"You needn't do that," I said. "I can just get something here at the hotel. What's the best way to get to the factory in the morning? Should I call a taxi? Rent a car?"

"I will pick you up each morning," Manuel said, smiling. "We are delighted to be your hosts," he added.

Hearing the phrase "delighted to be your hosts" was a new experience. People who run factories don't say stuff like this. Usually they say "Be there by six, six fifteen at the latest." If they are feeling unusually social they might say "There's a MacDonald's down the street." I thanked Manuel profusely and made more excuses for my lack of sociability. I was dog-tired from the overnight flight.

I slept for most of the afternoon, then crawled downstairs for a meal. A glance at the menu indicated that the hotel restaurant was trying too hard. I ordered the fish. It was excellent: simple but very fresh. I crawled back upstairs and sent some emails to indicate that I was alive. Then I spent some time looking up swear words in Portuguese, so that when I got to the processing plant I could understand what the real managers were saying.

Before passing out completely I tried to reach Paolo, but to no avail. I settled for sending him an email saying "miss you," and it was almost true. If I were awake, I surely would have missed him.

Cutrale has a big processing plant at the edge of town, and this is where Manuel took me every morning. I was assigned to work with an engineer named Alberto, who seemed endlessly amused that I was there to "consult" with him. It took several hours before I talked him into letting me look at the software running on the control system, and at the simulation of the new software he had prepared. It all looked pretty good. Finally I asked outright for something to do. Surely there was some task that needed a second person?

Alberto looked confused by this.

"You want to help with the installation?" Evidently this was a new idea. I explained that I thought that was what I was brought in to do. Alberto called his supervisor. After a short exchange, he closed the phone and looked at me.

"You are here as a consultant." I agreed with this. "My supervisor and the other managers just want you to observe the installation and some other aspects of the process. Then they will ask you some questions."

"Okay," I agreed, "but is there a shutdown planned for any point this week? When do you actually start using the new software?"

"Oh, it should take about five minutes on Thursday, if all goes well," he replied, "and you will be there. But now I am supposed to start showing you our facilities."

We put on our hard hats and steel-toed shoes. The first stop was the actual control room for the factory. I tried to conceal the surprise on my face. It reminded me of pictures I'd seen of air traffic control towers, with banks of computer monitors and a 360-degree view of the facilities. Stretching into the distance were citrus groves as far as I could see, except in the direction of the city.

"What do you think of our control room?" Alberto asked, smiling.

"Very impressive!" I didn't want to give away the fact that the only other citrus plant I had seen was miniscule by comparison. Alberto smiled, and pointed out one of the windows.

"That is the rail line. The plant backs right up to it and the cargo containers are lifted directly onto the flatbed rail cars."

"Most of your product is exported," I remarked pointlessly, having read this in the information packet Dan handed me.

"Virtually all of it," agreed Alberto, "and mostly to Europe as animal feed. The U.S. gets most of the juice, and the solids are processed into pellets, as I'm sure you know. Almost all of these go to Europe."

I already knew this, but I needed to behave as a good "consultant," so I asked more pointless questions as he gave me the tour. I had to admit, it was an impressive operation, as unlike the Florida plant as it could possibly be.

"Do you have problems with rats chewing the wires?" At this point I was just making conversation.

Alberto looked at me. I think he realized, at that moment, that I was actually an engineer like himself.

"We had that happen once. We will never use fiber optic cable again."

"Good decision," I agreed, "neither will the plant in Florida that I update once a year. Boy, did that smell bad."

"Did they make you clean it out?" There was a genuine tone of indignation in the question. I laughed.

"No. But that's because the main control operator there is a really nice person. If it weren't for him, I think the manager might have tried to make me do it."

"What's the name of the nice one?" Alberto asked, smiling politely.

"Carlos," I said. "I've known him for years. I look forward to that job every November."

"Why do they need you every year?" wondered Alberto. So I explained about the movement of gauges and sensors, about parts that break and unrecorded changes.

"Don't you have to update your system once a year and make sure that the control panels are corresponding to the right things?"

Alberto's jaw dropped.

"Um, no!" After a few moments he added, "Nobody would think of making an unrecorded change on the plant floor. It is unthinkable. It's never happened. My god, if something like that happened at least three people would end up fired."

At that moment I realized I had entered an alternate universe of Fully Functional Factories. I didn't know what they wanted me to do for them, but it was clear that they were going to educate me.

Later that evening I got Dan on videoconference. I told him how it was going, and described my confusion. He just shrugged. "Just try to give the customer what they seem to want," he advised. "There isn't much else we can do, is there?"

After half a week of being wined and dined and shown around like a visiting dignitary, I finally got Paolo on the phone.

"How is it going?" he inquired. "Is the job going to get done on time?"

I explained the general strangeness of the situation. I was having a pretty nice time of it, chatting endlessly with Alberto about the details of juice processing as practiced in Brazil versus south Florida. Other than the basic manufacturing process, the differences were myriad. Brazil usually looked a lot better by comparison.

"Do you want to meet me in Rio?" I was determined to spend a precious week of vacation in the famous city, with some excursions into the countryside. I was hoping for beaches, rainforest, and a certain handsome fellow to share it.

"Ah, Mimi," Paolo sighed, almost reproachfully, "It's such a long way to go for just a week. We should plan ahead and do it right—a real vacation for a whole month."

"But Paolo, I only get three weeks of vacation total. And I'm spending one next week. Oh, and there's tango in Rio. We could go dancing!" I was trying hard, perhaps too hard. I could feel Paolo's resistance.

"You make it sound wonderful," Paolo said agreeably. "I'll think about it."

We hung up. I uncapped one of the beers I had bought at the local grocery store and tried to drown my disappointment. I had no right to expect Paolo to pay for an expensive ticket and make such a long trip just to please me. But I have enough experience in relationships to know what "I'll think about it" means. It means no.

Tammy and I Skyped for an hour. She told me about her

frustration with her wedding plans. Her parents had agreed to pay for most of it. Tammy's mother, a socially ambitious size 5 megamom from an old Boston family, took this agreement as license to arrange every aspect of the event. Tammy and Steve were left in control of the exact wording of the vows. Tammy wanted blue; her mother wanted maroon. Tammy wanted an outdoor wedding in Vermont, her mother insisted on a particular church in Wellesley. Tammy wanted a soft jazz pianist, her mother wanted a distant cousin who would play Chopin. Tammy and Steve both wanted to have a friend perform the ceremony, but all four parents insisted on a "legitimate" clergyman associated with the particular church in Wellesley.

"Whose wedding is it, anyway!" Tammy complained to me—the complaint of every bride since Eve, I was sure.

"Well, a wedding is a social contract," I offered, hoping to sooth her anxieties, "and so, in a sense, it doesn't belong just to the bride and groom."

"So what are you advising, exactly?" She was a bit testy, and I was trying to tread softly. This is not my strong suit.

"I guess I'm advising that your life will be easier if you just let your mom have her way," I said, adding, "and then go have a really good honeymoon and get over it?"

"My mother said you shouldn't be a bridesmaid!"

"Them's fightin' words!" I laughed, "I hope you got your way on that one!"

"Indeed, I did," Tammy smiled into the camera.

The conversation turned to how my trip to Brazil

was progressing. I told Tammy about my strange role as "consultant," and being treated like an Important Person, a role to which I was not accustomed. Tammy got this expression on her face, an expression I recognized. Her antennae were out.

"They want something from you," she said. "What do you think it is?"

"I can't imagine," I replied, "I'm no investor, and they don't need engineers here. They have plenty. Education is free here. There are loads of engineers of every kind. I can't imagine what I might have to offer."

Tammy looked thoughtful. "Call me tomorrow. I'm really curious what they are going to ask you after the shutdown. When do you go to Rio? Is Paolo coming?"

"Saturday. I don't think so." At this I must have looked tearful.

"Oh, Mimi, it's just such a long way for only a week. Don't expect that, it's just too much. What are you going to do in Rio?"

That was a good question. I had three guidebooks, and had done some scouting on the Internet. If you want to see rainforest, you have to leave Rio. But it looked like it was worth spending time in the city also.

"I'm spending three days in Rio, then four days in a little B&B in the country northeast of Rio. Then another two nights in Rio, then home."

"Wow," said Tammy, somewhat enviously, "Where did you find the B&B?"

"Online," I confessed, "and they'll pick me up and take me there. It's an expensive ride, but an inexpensive hotel. They'll feed me, too. I'm not sure what to expect, but I'd like to get out of the city and see the countryside. And I'm hoping to see the rainforest. Darwin was there. I want to see what he saw."

"You are a true geek," Tammy said appreciatively. "Will there be monkeys?"

"Wow, I dunno!" I hadn't really thought about the monkey question. It cheered me up. "The people that own the place are German. I don't know why they moved to Brazil. I wonder what the neighborhood will be like. I don't think it's near the beach."

This pretty much exhausted my knowledge of the week to come. I just hadn't had enough time to make proper plans and research a good vacation. I was throwing myself into something without much advance planning. It felt good. It felt like an adventure.

"By the way," said Tammy, "I talked to Todd. That dress you wore at Lu's wedding? I told him not to dye it. If my mother has her way, all of you will be dressed like maroon munchkins at the munchkin prom. So I told him to hold off. I'm not sure I'll win this one."

"I wish you the very best of luck!" I said, completely honestly. At this moment, my lace dress was the furthest thing from my mind. Unless I could tango with Paolo in it, it had no meaning for me. And, hanging up on Tammy, I felt lonely and sad, even with the prospect of brilliant Rio de Janeiro before me.

Thursday's shutdown went without a single hitch. Alberto loaded the new software, started it up, the place shut down, the connections were re-set and the system rebooted. Production resumed with hardly any delay. In all my years in the industry, I had never seen such a smooth a transition after an upgrade.

"Miss Mimi," the senior engineer said, "What do you think of our operation?"

We were at lunch Friday at a fairly fancy place downtown. Claudio, the senior engineer, and two other managers, asked me endless questions.

"How does our restart compare with your experience at the Florida plant?"

"How many years have you consulted at the Florida plant?"

"Can you think of any way we could improve our operation?"

"Can the control operator in the Florida plant see what is going on in other parts? Or does he rely on the phone?"

"Intercom," I replied. "It's an older system, but it works. No, he can't see as well as your operators can."

"How long is downtime at that plant?"

"This year we were down half a day for repairs all around, all simultaneously, not just the control system," I replied.

"Alberto said you mentioned monkeys. Do monkeys get into the plant there?"

I had to laugh. Alberto misunderstood the reference. I tried to explain how stuff got moved around during the year, and how I compared it to monkeys meddling with the works. My hosts looked appalled.

"But Mimi, why would anybody change the location of a sensor or a gauge, without recording it?"

"Beats me," I said. The more I thought about it, the weirder it seemed. Why do we settle for such half-hearted imprecision and sloppiness in our factories? Why do the people who work there promote sloppiness as an aesthetic choice? It was a mystery. I turned the question on its head. "Why are the Brazilian engineers so meticulous?"

My hosts all looked at me in wonderment. "What good is a sloppy engineer?" Claudio said, evidently speaking for all of them. "If someone behaves like that, we fire them and get somebody who pays attention."

"I think that is the problem," I said. "We have trouble replacing our engineers. Not so many people want the job, or are qualified to do it."

My hosts thought about this, and had a lot to say as well, although it was all in Portuguese. Conversation was intense, incomprehensible, animated. After several minutes, they seemed to realize that I was watching and clearly wondering what was going on.

"Excuse us," Claudio said, "but we were surprised by your answer. But if you don't mind, Alberto said you worked with one good worker at the Florida plant. Is it true? Or was he just the least bad?" I explained about Carlos and my annual visits.

The next day, as I boarded the plane from São Paolo to Rio, I was still wondering what the purpose was of my visit, and whether the customer was pleased.

Dan insisted on a Skype meeting the day I got to Rio.

139

Evidently he was as perplexed about my visit to Cutrale as I was. We talked for half an hour. I'm pretty sure he was even more confused when we were done. I managed to reach Paolo, who was on his way out the door but spared a few minutes to say hello and ask how it was going. I hadn't been able to reach him all week, and was curious to know what he would make of the situation at Cutrale. But he seemed to be in a great hurry, and promised we would Skype the next day. I was lounging on the small rooftop terrace of the modest bed and breakfast I had booked. Everything about it was cute but the view over the rooftops of Rio was spectacular. I didn't care to wander the streets of Rio alone at night, so I picked up dinner to go and a few beers. I watched the sun set over the rooftops while I ate and drank myself into a state of pleasant relaxation.

Then I Skyped Tammy. Her wedding was just a few weeks away, and she was looking a little frayed around the edges. I asked if she was okay, and she looked like she might cry.

"If it were just my mother telling me what to do, it would be okay," she explained, "but having two mothers tell you what to do is impossible! When they disagree, they put me in the middle. So then I try to get an opinion from Steve, who tries not to give one. Some days I'm mad at all three of them. Why is it so important where the flowers come from or what kind of cake? I mean, why is it important to them? I know why it's important to me."

"Hmmm," I said sympathetically, "and how is the dress coming?"

"Neither of them liked the dress, but it was too late."

"Good," I said. "Maybe that's a strategy you could

use with other decisions, too. What all still has to be decided?"

"Cake. Flowers. Favors. Wine for the dinner. Champagne for the toast. Music, if any, and I do want some. At least we have the basic ceremony and reception figured out. It's just a few more things but it's driving me nuts."

"How about a divide and conquer strategy?" I offered. "Put one mother in charge of the cake. Put the other in charge of flowers and favors. Get Tanner to pick wine and champagne—he's great at it! But do NOT take his advice on music. What kind of music do you want?"

"Oh, something pleasant and not loud, on a real instrument. Don't tell me. You want tango, right?"

"No, I wasn't going to suggest that. It's not quite light enough. But what about some soft Irish music? If you go to the pub where Andy and I always went you could ask the musicians there if they know anybody who would like to play for a wedding."

"Oh, right. Bagpipes. Just what every wedding needs!" Tammy giggled at the prospect.

"No, silly," I laughed, "flute and violin. Ask for O'Carolan tunes. They are lovely, and there are plenty of waltzes for the new couple to dance. Get somebody soon. Otherwise you're going to wind up with somebody's cousin Vinnie playing the theme from Romeo and Juliet. Which will segue into "Nights in White Satin," and end with "Some Enchanted Evening." Unless you can get the Boston Pops to play that stuff for your wedding, I think an Irish set would be better. How refreshing not to recognize every single tune."

Tammy admitted I had a point, but said, "Actually,

my cousin Mary Ellen offered to play piano for the wedding and the reception. She's pretty good, but I have to admit she did mention Romeo and Juliet. I'll think about it."

I had my doubts that she would bother to get anybody besides cousin Mary Ellen. There is just too much to arrange for a wedding, and I could see it would be a relief to see one more thing settled.

"I sent an invitation to Tanner," Tammy continued, "over the objections of both mothers, as they had never met him. I explained that he helped me pick out the dress. Somehow this didn't make it easier. But I figured that since you would be bringing Paolo, Tanner needed his own invitation."

"Thanks!" I had overlooked that consequence. "That's so thoughtful," I added, "especially considering all the stuff you have to plan."

"So," Tammy steered the conversation away from endless wedding considerations, "What is Paolo up to while you are gone? Is he going to meet you in Rio?"

"I don't know. I haven't been able to talk to him for any length of time, and I only managed to reach him once last week. And when I invited him to come meet me, he wouldn't say yes or no. I think he was just too polite to say no."

Tammy was silent. This is never a good sign. She studied my face on the screen.

"What?" I said. "Should I worry?"

"Have you texted him?" She asked. "Have you sent him a sexy note or anything? Do you know if he is in Port Charlotte, or Boston, or somewhere else?"

"Well, no," I said, and in my defense: "They kept me pretty busy at the plant."

"Mimi," Tammy said, suddenly troubled, "Tanner sent me a picture from his phone. Paolo was at a milonga in Medford this weekend. He said he came to run a tango workshop."

"He didn't tell me that!" Now I was troubled too. Where did he stay? I would have let him use my apartment, although it wasn't particularly close to Medford.

"Tanner said Paolo was staying with friends," Tammy the mind reader replied. Somehow this was not reassuring. Paolo knew a lot of the Boston dancers, many of whom I considered to be romantic rivals, judging from their behavior at the dances. I didn't believe for a minute that Tanner let that pass without asking questions, and I said so.

"I guess Paolo just didn't want to tell him where he was staying," said Tammy, "and I wonder why not. Tanner also asked if Paolo was going to meet you in Rio."

"What did he say?" I asked, the pit of my stomach suddenly knotted. Tammy hesitated.

"He said he didn't think so."

I couldn't look at Tammy. I stared at my hands. Of course I knew he wasn't going to come. But I guess I hadn't given up hope completely. The sensation of giving up hope completely is not pleasant.

"Thanks for telling me," I lied. "I guess I'll find out what happened when I get back."

"Mimi," Tammy said sternly, "you should talk to

him. Send a text. Make it sexy. Get his attention, and then talk to him."

"Okay," I agreed weakly.

"Tonight. Text him tonight." When Tammy gets serious like this, it is pointless to disobey.

"I will," I said meekly, knowing that if I didn't, somehow Tammy would be able to tell.

"Good girl," Tammy smiled. "Just keep reminding him that you're in love. Better yet, remind him that he's in love."

We signed off and I turned to finish the last few bites of my dinner. The fish, beans and rice were now the same temperature as the beer, a balmy seventy-five degrees.

~~Crazy about you.~~

~~Miss you.~~

~~Miss you tonight.~~

~~Miss you 2nite.~~

~~Need your loving.~~

~~Need your lovin'.~~

~~Need you.~~

~~Can't wait to see you again.~~

~~Miss you please call.~~

Crazy here without you.

Rio lovely but not so much without you. Sigh.

Wish we could share this gorgeous sunset.

Want to see you so bad.

Crazy jealous girlfriend wants to know where you have been?

Long nights without you.

How could it take three hours to compose a single sentence of text? And why am I so bad at romantic messages? And what did Tammy have in mind when she said that I should remind him that he loves me?

Dreaming of you holding me.

Thinking of your touch.

Missing that connection. Let's dance.

Hmmm. Maybe I should go for something a bit more overt. I found the list of sext slang. Disgusting, basically. No, Paolo is too classy for that junk. I hope!

Do you miss me? You are supposed to miss me!

What I want right now is only you.

These are getting worse and worse. I could get a job with a greeting card company. What's wrong with just plain honesty?

How did your workshop go? I miss you.

I took a taxi to the bottom of a gondola lift, just a few blocks from the ocean. The gondola takes you up to the top of Sugarloaf, a mountain jutting straight up out of the sea. From the top, all of Rio is visible. Informal housing crawled up the steep mountainsides that cradled the downtown. Ships crowded the harbor. The wind whipped my hair into a mess.

Walking to the other side of the platform, a view of Copacabana beach stretched into the distance. A nice long walk on a sandy beach sounded like the perfect way to spend my day in Rio. A tourist and her husband posed for pictures. He took one of her, then he handed her the camera.

"Would you like me to take your picture together?" I asked.

They posed for me, with the stunning view of mountains and beaches stretching into the distance behind them. When they were satisfied with the picture, I handed them my cell phone and stood in the same spot. Later, as I rode the gondola back down, I realized that at last I had the perfect message for Paolo. I sent him the picture of me, smiling into the camera, with a world-class view behind me, and wind whipping my hair about. This is me. This is where I am. Where are you? But no words were needed.

The confusions and uncertainties of the past week had taken their toll on me. I needed the universal antidote to stress and trouble: sunshine, exercise, and good food. I took a taxi to the Copacabana beach. For the rest of the day I walked the length of it, many times. I walked barefoot in the salt water. I watched the soccer-volley players expertly lob soccer balls over a volleyball net with their feet, heads, and chest. It was impressive. I walked along the street and investigated every booth selling beer and snacks. I counted the fishing boats at the far end of the beach. I had lunch at a tiny street counter a block away from the beach, serving fish that was so fresh it must have been caught that morning. I ate surrounded by working men on their lunch break. I investigated the neighborhoods. In the early evening I ate fried manioc as a snack, accompanied by chopp, a draft beer. I picked a restaurant near the beach for dinner, and ate a horrible reheated and overly sauced piece of meat. I found a music store and, to my surprise, within it was a jazz band playing soft sambas. I stayed to listen. Finally, exhausted, I caught a taxi to my little hotel.

Arriving at my room, I checked the computer. I opened Skype. Nobody was online. I looked at my email. No word from Paolo. But there was a note from Tanner:

> **Todd and I went to a milonga this weekend. Guess who was there? Our very own Paolo! And my, he was popular. He seems to be staying with a friend, not quite sure what the relationship is. He said he was in town to teach a private tango workshop. Don't panic. But you better ask some questions.**

Once again I found myself on a beautiful terrace overlooking Rio, with a beer in my hand. I sat near the edge, with my back to the terrace. I drank in the view, all sparkly lights and water, and quietly cried.

The day before I left Brazil, Paolo finally picked up my Skype call.

"Mimi, how are you? Are you enjoying Brazil? Where are you now?"

Frankly, it was hard to know where to start. It was hard to look completely happy. The simplest course of action was just to answer the question.

"I'm in Saquarema, a little town outside Rio, in a cattle ranching region. I'm in a tiny B&B in the middle of basically nowhere, but it's paradise. Can you hear the monkeys screaming?"

"No," he admitted, "not from here. It sounds wonderful though."

"Tanner said he saw you at a milonga in Medford."

"Yes," said Paolo, perhaps a bit warily, "I was surprised to see him. I guess I shouldn't have been, but I was."

"Paolo," I said, cutting to the chase, "is everything alright?"

He averted his eyes from the camera. He sighed thoughtfully.

"Well, Mimi, to be honest, I've been thinking." I said nothing, waiting for him to continue. "Mimi, you know I love you."

I smiled weakly. Under other circumstances I would have been delighted to hear it.

"I love you too," I answered, adding honestly, "and I've missed you terribly."

Paolo sighed again. "Look, I just wonder if it can ever work out between us, with our complicated lives. When you wanted me to go with you to Brazil, I thought about it for a long time. You want to travel, and have adventures. And so, I guess, do I. But if we are both

148

determined to have adventures, as well as work that takes us here and there, maybe it's better if we remain open to other options."

"What do you mean?" I asked stupidly, knowing full well what he meant.

"Oh, Mimi," he said, "you know what I mean."

Tanner said "don't panic." But I panicked. And I hung up.

I went outside and listened to the monkeys calling in the night. I walked around the little garden and sniffed at the flowers. I put on my swimsuit and swam laps in the pool. I went to the little bar and ordered a caipirinha. I took it to my room and drank it. I resisted the urge to have a second one. When I finally stopped crying, I called Paolo back. Thankfully, he answered.

"Paolo, I'm sorry for hanging up on you."

"It's okay, I understand."

"I'm coming home tomorrow."

"I know."

"Which means I'll really be home day after tomorrow."

"I know."

"Where are you now?"

"I'm at home in Port Charlotte."

"Can I come and see you? I'll get off the plane in Miami. I'll rent a car and drive over."

Paolo sighed.

"Mimi, you don't have to do this."

"Yes, I do."

"In that case," he said with a tone of resignation, "I will be at the airport to pick you up. You will be in no shape to drive."

I blew a kiss to Paolo, almost crying. I sent an email to Dan, explaining that I might be delaying my return for a day or two. I packed my bags in preparation for the next day. I set the alarm. I took a shower, crawled into the bed, and cried myself to sleep.

CHAPTER 6

"Let's not talk about it yet," Paolo gently insisted, closing the car door.

So we didn't. He asked about my trip, showing a studied interest in every detail, including aspects of citrus processing that even I found boring.

"You are asking as many questions as they did!" I laughed, starting to relax in spite of myself. "The types of extractions, cold pressing, steam extraction; they asked a million questions. I had to admit I only knew how things were done at one plant, but I assumed they were standard processes. Once or twice they looked a little surprised at something. I had to keep saying, "I'm just the control engineer!"

"Maybe they want to learn about new methods."

"Oh, I don't think so. I've never seen a slicker, more modern factory than the one in Brazil." It was time to turn the conversation to a less comfortable, but to me more important, topic. "How did your tango workshop go? And how did it come to happen?"

"Oh, well, you know that I started to tango when I was still living in Boston. And because of you, I once again was in touch with a few of the people I knew then. When they found out about all the training and work I've done since then, they asked me to run a workshop."

"Why did you do it while I was gone?"

Paolo now looked uncomfortable.

"Well, it was sort of a private, high-end workshop. There are some very competitive dancers in Boston, as you well know. They got together and talked me into it."

"They didn't want me there."

"No," Paolo admitted, "they didn't want anybody there but them."

"How many people were in the group?"

"Five."

"Five couples?"

"No, Mimi," Paolo looked sideways at me as he drove. "Three women and two men. I was the third man dancing."

"Tell me more," I said, leaving the direction open. Paolo sighed again and looked sideways at me as he drove.

"Well, I don't suppose you have ever heard of Cygne Rouge? I didn't think so. Only a few people have heard of it, and they like to keep it that way. Basically, it's a milonga. But it happens only once every other year, and attendance is by invitation only. They charge around five thousand dollars per person for the weekend, and use a grand hotel in a different city each time."

"Have you ever gone?"

"No," Paolo said, "but I almost went once. I was dancing with Lourdes, do you remember her?"

Oh yes, I thought, I remember her. She was all over Paolo from the minute he showed up at the Boston dance. I nodded.

"Well, we were invited about ten years ago. But Lourdes had the bad taste to fall in love with someone. He didn't dance and was too jealous to let us go to the event without him. So, alas, neither of us went."

"Was Lourdes one of the people at the workshop?"

"Yes."

"Is she the one who needs a partner?"

"Yes. She received another invitation to attend with Moses Cantor as her partner. They accepted, but then Moses fell ill. He had an operation, there were complications, and he just can't go."

"How do they know who to invite?"

"Oh, the top tango dancers all know of each other. There are enough competitions and international workshops and so on; they just know. And for each Cygne Rouge event, they pick exactly twenty couples. It's very secretive. No one knows who organizes the event. And they also get the best musicians from around the world. I've heard the music is amazing."

"Cool," I admitted, "but why?"

"Mimi, when you get to be really good at something,

sometimes it's nice just to immerse yourself in the dance, and not have to worry about teaching anybody anything, or dancing with all your students, or switching partners. At Cygne Rouge you just go with your one partner and dance all night."

"People don't change partners?"

"No. Most of them are professionals, and many are competition dancers with their longtime partner. This year it's in Ljubljana, the capital of Slovenia. The guidebook calls it "Little Prague." It's supposed to be lovely."

I had to admit, I was liking it less and less. Paolo was going off to someplace with a women who flirts with him constantly, in order to dance the sexiest dance on earth in the classiest, and probably most romantic, venue in existence. Just for the experience. Right.

"I feel like Lourdes's jealous boyfriend."

"I'm not surprised. I'm afraid there is one other thing you aren't going to like. Cygne Rouge is exactly the week of Tammy's wedding."

"No!" Misery comes in many forms. There's the fear of losing someone you love, the anger at feeling cheated, frustration at not being good enough at something, disappointment at being stood up for an important date. All of these converged inside me.

"Well, I could get back the day before the wedding, and still be your date. But I have a feeling you might not want me there."

"I take it you said yes to all of this."

"Yes. I said yes."

Dinner was strained, with both of us trying to talk about everything except what was important. When we got to his house, Paolo opened a bottle of wine and offered me a glass. I took it, gladly.

He put his arm around me, gingerly, as if it were our first date all over again. I snuggled in instinctively, knowing full well that tenderness can be faked and if so, in the end would be no consolation at all. We said nothing, and my mind went in all directions at once. Had he slept with Lourdes? Was he planning to do so? Was Cygne Rouge a one-time opportunity or the start of a new direction for him? After two glasses of wine, I could no longer suppress my thoughts.

"So what exactly did you mean when you said we should keep our options open?"

"Oh, Mimi." Paolo looked at me. "It means what it sounds like. I love you. But I'm not sure we were meant to be together, and I knew you weren't going to like being left out of my workshop, the trip to Slovenia, all that. I don't want to make you feel deserted, but it just is what it is. So if someone comes along that is easier for you to be with, or doesn't make you feel insecure by doing what I'm about to do, then you should be open to such an option."

"Should I feel insecure?" This was, after all, the crux of the question.

"At this point, no," Paolo said gently, "but I don't know what will happen between Lourdes and me. I certainly don't intend to be her lover, but frankly she is working pretty hard at making that happen. And she has offered me now the one thing I have wanted to do for so long."

Suddenly something became clear.

"You don't have to pay for the trip with sex," I said flatly.

"Oh, I didn't mean that," Paolo said, looking a bit taken aback. "I just meant that in situations like that, stuff happens. Twelve straight hours of tango, all night, in a beautiful ballroom with a beautiful woman. Think about it. I'm not superhuman and I don't want to make a promise I might not be able to keep. And I don't want to lie to you about it either."

I pondered this and drank more wine.

"Surely you have had lots of chances to be this woman's lover in the past."

"Well, I suppose so. But sometimes I was in a relationship myself, and sometimes I was preoccupied with work." Paolo looked up at the ceiling. "And then, frankly, she kind of scares me."

"What do you mean?"

"Well, she has the fancy job, the perfect house, the gorgeous body, expensive clothes, and she wants the perfect dance partner for a boyfriend. I'm not sure I want that role. But that was ten years ago, and maybe she has mellowed."

I hoped not. If Paolo thought he could have two girlfriends at the same time, he was wrong—at least if he wanted me to be one of them.

"I'm not into sharing you."

"I understand. Mimi, whatever you decide is okay. If you don't want to sleep with me tonight, I understand completely. Really I do."

"Oh no," I said, looking him in the eye, "I fully intend to seduce you tonight. And as many nights as I can before you go to Cygne Rouge. And I hope you will still escort me to Tammy's wedding. But here's the deal. After her wedding I'm going to ask you some questions. Everything after that depends on how you answer them. Understood?"

Paolo held my gaze for a long time. I broke eye contact, and shifted my gaze to the window. Paolo sniffed his wine.

"Wow," Paolo took a sip of wine, then another. "Just wow."

I took his wine away and crawled into his lap. We kissed intensely. He slowly unbuttoned my shirt, then rose and led me to the bedroom.

The best kind of despair is passionate despair.

It was a long night. We made love until we exhausted ourselves completely. All of my fears and hopes merged into a single dark passion, and I became a demanding lover. Paolo met all demands, at the same time gentle and fierce. We collapsed into deep sleep around four a.m. and slept soundly until the doorbell rang.

Paolo threw on some clothes and went down to answer it. He was gone for a while. I rolled over and went back to sleep. After some time I felt him sit down next to me. He put his hand on my shoulder.

"Mimi, wake up."

"Do I have to?"

"Yes, I think so. Wake up and put some clothes on. There is a man downstairs who wants to talk to you."

"Seriously?" I answered. "Who?"

"I think it's best if you are prompt. His name is Frank Stevens."

"I don't know any such person."

"I know." Paolo looked at me intently. "But you must talk with him now."

I put on some jeans and the last clean shirt in my suitcase. Paolo escorted me downstairs. The visitor was waiting politely in the living room, sitting on the sofa. He rose when I came in.

"Are you Miranda Darrow?"

"Yes," I said, shaking his hand. He pulled out his wallet and opened it.

"Frank Stevens," he said. "I'm with the FBI." He showed me his identification card. "May I ask you a few questions?"

"Um," I stammered, taken completely off guard, "I suppose so, sure. What is this about?"

Frank Stevens addressed Paolo. "Is there somewhere we could speak privately?"

"Of course," Paolo replied, "you can use my study." He led us there. "If you would like a cup of tea or coffee, please let me know," he said, shutting the door behind him. Frank Stevens and I looked at each other and smiled uncomfortable smiles.

"Miss Darrow," he began, taking out a small laptop and preparing to take notes, "Is it true that you work for Controltech Corporation?"

"Yes," I confirmed. "I have worked there for six years."

"How well do you know Mr. John Smith?"

"Ah, Tanner. I've known Tanner since I started working there."

"Tanner? Ah yes, John Tanner Smith. Are you strictly work acquaintances, or do you know him socially?"

"He is a friend," I answered, becoming suspicious, "a good friend." I wondered what Tanner could possibly have done to have the FBI tracking him.

"Did he recently do a job for your company at King Citrus in South Florida?"

"Yes," I replied, "he worked with me on that job. I was there for almost three weeks, and Tanner came for the last week or so. What is this about, Mr. Stevens?"

"I will tell you presently. But first, what do you know about d-limonene?"

There wasn't much to know in my estimation. "It's a by-product of citrus juice and is the basis for cleaning agents used commercially and in households. You can buy stuff in the grocery store that is made with it. Smells like oranges, which is nice."

"Do you know how it is extracted?"

"Well, there are two main methods, cold and hot. You can use a centrifuge or you can distill it with steam." This was a very strange question from the FBI. Surely they could have just asked the manufacturers.

"Are you aware of any other methods?"

"No," I said, pondering. Then a small light bulb went off. "Wait, the plant in Florida recently got some new machinery. It's not up and running yet, but it's supposed to be a d-limonene extractor. I started working on the control system for it, but since it's a fairly self-contained item, I don't know much about how it works, exactly."

"Do you know why the plant purchased it?"

"I guess it makes a higher grade product. I really don't know."

"Do you know who makes it?"

"Oh"—I tried to remember—"Emulso, maybe? No, some place I haven't heard of. Extenda. Yes, that's it. Why are you asking me these questions? I'm sure the plant would tell you what they bought." Stevens looked annoyed.

"Miss Darrow," he continued, "Did you recently do a job for Cutrale Industries in Brazil?"

"Yes." This was getting stranger by the minute.

"And was Mr. Smith with you on that job?"

"No."

"Thank you." He typed some notes on his laptop.

Then he looked at me.

"What exactly was the job you did for Cutrale?"

Unfortunately, I still hadn't figured out the answer to that question. I couldn't imagine why the FBI would care what I had done there. I decided to tell Stevens what the people at Cutrale kept telling me.

"I was a consultant."

"What, exactly, did you consult on?"

"They asked me my opinion about lots of things in their factory. Which was a very impressive operation, by the way. Really, they kind of grilled me."

Stevens looked at me thoughtfully.

"Do you work exclusively on citrus plants?"

"Oh, no," I replied, "we work on all kinds of manufacturing plants, but only on the control systems. Paper mills, ethanol plants, insecticide plants, biofuel, cereal, . . ." Stevens cut me off.

"Why would they hire an American control engineer as a general consultant to a citrus plant in Brazil?" He looked intently at me, as if sure that I would know the answer.

I sighed. "I wish I knew." I looked at him, shrugging. "Can you please tell me what this is about?"

"Yes. One more question though. Did anyone in Brazil ask you for details about the plant in Florida?"

I felt the panic rising in me. They had asked endless questions about the Florida plant. Suddenly their questions seemed less innocent. I started to sweat. Lying was a useless strategy. I'm a lousy liar.

"Yes," I answered flatly, "now tell me what this is about."

Frank Stevens looked at me, weighing his words. He looked at his laptop and made a few more notes. He exhaled deeply.

"The executives at King Citrus believe that Cutrale is conducting a form of industrial espionage on the company. They believe they have evidence that someone is leaking information, in particular about their new d-limonene extractor, to a rival foreign company. They asked us to investigate, and our investigations led to you. You are the only person to have spent time at both plants. They thought it might be you or Mr. Smith. But several people now have assured me that Smith was not at Cutrale, nor has he spoken with them. Thus, you are the prime suspect."

He waited for a response. I thought about it.

"I don't think I said anything they didn't already know. The same citrus extraction processes are used by almost everybody in the industry. I knew they had the new d-limonene extractor, but there wasn't much I could say about it. They did pump me on it, though."

Frank Stevens stood up.

"Thank you, Miss Darrow. You have been very cooperative. I don't know whether King Citrus will press charges. It will be difficult for them to sue Cutrale, as it is not a U.S. company. They may choose to sue Controltech, or they may choose to sue you. It remains to be seen. I have made a note that you have been extremely cooperative in this investigation. If you are sued, the judge may decide that you acted in ignorance rather than malice.

I am asking you to continue to cooperate by not mentioning our conversation to anyone except perhaps your attorney until charges are brought, if indeed they are."

"My attorney! I don't have an attorney!" I had never needed a lawyer for anything.

"Well, I suggest you find one, just in case. And here is my card," he added, handing me a business card with only a name and telephone number on it. "Call if you have any questions."

With that, Frank Stevens rose and left.

Paolo found me slumped on the sofa, crying again but for a whole new reason.

"I don't suppose you can tell me what that was about."

"No!" I said, crying more loudly. "I'm not supposed to."

I looked at him.

"Don't worry," he said, "I heard most of it anyway. It's our secret. Shh," he continued, kissing me lightly, "don't worry. It won't do any good."

"It's the slickest, most modern food processing plant I've ever seen."

Now Dan was pumping me about Cutrale. What did they want from us? What did I do for them? What did I work on? Were they planning to use our services in the future? All of these questions are normal after a trip to a new client. Dan would of course want to add a client to our customer base, and Cutrale was a big fish. If they had us do work for them it could potentially be a big windfall for the company. But now I was seeing other, less friendly, motives in Dan's questions.

"What extraction processes do they use for d-limonene?" Dan smiled as he asked this. I had the impression that he was trying very hard to look relaxed. Dan has never done a job at King Citrus or any other food processing plant. His background is more about oil refineries and ethanol production. He never showed much curiosity about citrus processing, except in regard to the software controlling the various parts of the plant. I smiled back, trying to look relaxed too.

"They use both cold press and steam extraction, depending on what its final use will be. Steam distillation gives a product that is used in commercial cleaners. Cold extraction can give a food grade product with some processes. Exactly what they have for extractors I'm not sure. We didn't get into that. Why do you ask?"

I just wanted to see his reaction. It was thinly masked alarm. I realized that someone from the FBI must have questioned him also, as the company was a potential subject for a lawsuit. I had promised not to talk about my conversation with Frank Stevens, but I did not promise to keep my employers ignorant of my trip to Brazil.

"I didn't give away any trade secrets," I told Dan bluntly. "Their operation is very smooth, and I don't know enough about the details of citrus processing to be useful in that regard. Whether they were trying to get information from me is another thing entirely. They certainly asked a million questions."

Dan looked at me carefully.

"So the FBI has talked with you."

"I'm not free to talk about it."

Dan thought about this for a minute. It was a very uncomfortable minute, during which I realized that there were more options than I had considered up to this point. I could be sued. I could be fired. I could be sued and fired. I liked Dan, and didn't think he would be inclined to fire me, but he might decide it was necessary. I decided to rely on more bluntness.

"Are you going to fire me?"

Dan raised his eyebrows as if the thought was just now occurring to him. At this moment, I knew for certain I was an idiot. He didn't answer. He drummed his fingers on the table and stared past me out the window. Finally he spoke.

"It's not an impossible outcome, Mimi," he said carefully, "but it depends on what happens next."

The stress of the past few weeks got the better of me. Normally I would never show anger or frustration at work. I threw Dan's words back in his face.

"Please remember that my boss said: 'Try to give the customer what they seem to want.' That's what my boss said, and that's exactly what I tried to do. Fortunately my ignorance probably kept me from giving them everything they wanted. If, in fact, there was something inappropriate that they wanted, which is not an established fact. But I did my best to obey orders."

Dan's eyes narrowed. "You're saying we're in this together. Which I suppose is correct, although if I fired you we'd be less together."

"It would be an admission of guilt. I don't think it would help your case."

"Or yours."

"Do you think I intentionally gave away private information?"

"You intentionally gave away information. Whether it was private will be up to the court to decide. Do I believe you intended to act as a corporate spy? No, of course not." Dan looked at me kindly.

"Thank you," I said. Dan took out a notebook and copied some information onto a piece of paper, which he handed me.

"This is our lawyer," he said, "but you can't use her. It might be a conflict of interest. This second person is another lawyer who handled a case for a friend of mine. He was pretty good. You might want to get in touch."

"You really think I need a lawyer?"

"Mimi, the penalty for corporate espionage can be twenty years in prison."

"Thanks," I said, diving into despair.

"Mimi," Dan continued, "Take a few days off. Please. Compose yourself and make a plan."

"Thanks," I said weakly, trying not to cry. I left the office a few minutes later, went home, and fell completely to pieces.

I did not, however, call the lawyer Dan suggested. That evening Paolo tried to talk me down from my panic.

"Never use the lawyer suggested by someone with a competing interest. Dan's a nice guy, and he wants you to have a good lawyer. But he does not want you to have a better lawyer than the company has. When push comes to shove, he would much rather you take the blame."

"Well then, how shall I find a good lawyer?"

Paolo smiled over Skype. "I have already found him."

I smiled back bleakly. I adored him, and trusted him. And then I thought of Lourdes and his upcoming trip with her, and my stomach hurt.

"I had to sue someone over intellectual property a few years ago," Paolo continued, "and a lot was at stake: the loss of my entire income, for starters. My business partner and I did a lot of research before settling on this person, and he did an excellent job. He is expensive, however, so you don't want to use him unnecessarily. I told him to look into the situation but not spend more than a day on it until you are actually charged with something."

"Dan told me to take a few days off."

"Oh dear. That is not a good sign. Tell you what, why don't you come down here for a few days?"

"But I'm a wreck." I didn't want my stressed state of mind to interfere with my attempts to impress Paolo with my ardor.

"I know." He smiled, saying, "I love you even when you're a wreck. Pack up, fly today."

So I did. On the way to the airport there were two texts. One was from Tanner, asking why I left work early. He wanted to have lunch, find out about the trip to Brazil, hear about my adventures in Rio. I replied that I had a headache. Tammy texted, wanting to go out to a movie just to get a respite from the wedding plans. I replied that I was taking a few days off work and heading to Florida to see Paolo. This was followed by a concerned reply. *Is everything alright?* There was only one honest answer to that. *No. Talk later.*

Paolo took one look at me and drove us directly to the beach. We walked barefoot for an hour, holding each other close. I cried and told him what Dan had said about a twenty-year prison sentence.

"Tonight you must eat well, sleep well, and relax. Tomorrow you are going to tell me everything you remember about what happened at Cutrale and what you told them. I will take notes and prepare a complete description. Believe me, thoroughness and honesty are what will save you."

"Okay," I agreed, "but I don't know if I can relax. I find the whole situation so unbelievable. I can't even imagine what trade secrets King Citrus could possibly have. As far as I know, they don't build any of their own equipment. They just buy it. So what could the big secret be?"

"Well, maybe they just don't want their competitors to know what exactly they own. Maybe they feel that their assemblage of equipment is somehow private information. They did recently buy some fancy new extractors."

"How would you know that?" I looked at Paolo, who had an amused smile on his face.

"Tango teachers know more than you might expect," he grinned, "especially if they can learn from their students."

"Carlos!"

"Yes, I had a few conversations discretely with Carlos."

"But he could get into trouble too!"

"I suspect he already is in trouble. After all, he was the one working with you. Were you aware that there is almost entirely new management at King Citrus?"

"Yes, he mentioned that in November. It didn't sound like he liked them. But he also didn't deal with them much."

"Yes, it was part of the process of their IPO. Now they are a publicly owned company. The former owner retired, holding only twenty percent of the shares, and installed an executive management team to take his place. None of this is private information. You can go buy stock in King Citrus online now. I'll tell you more about it tomorrow. Tonight, please forget about your troubles if you can."

With that, he stepped in front of me and took me in close embrace. He walked me backwards down the beach, a slow tango walk, humming a favorite melody softly in my ears. I felt my blood pressure drop, felt myself melt happily into the dance. After a good while, he paused, and kissed me.

"May I take you to dinner?" He smiled his most winning smile.

"It would be a pleasure."

We spent the whole day going over what happened at Cutrale. Paolo took notes, asking about every person I spent time with, recording whatever I remembered about what they asked and what I answered. Whenever I got worked up about the whole thing, and upset, we would stop for a bit. Three times we ended up in the bedroom. Four times we made meals and snacks. When I felt calm we would recommence the memory exercise.

"Okay, we are done with this for today," Paolo announced late in the afternoon. "You've had enough and we will do more tomorrow. "

"But I've told you everything," I protested.

"Ah, but there are other questions that need to be asked. For now though, we are done. Let's shower and go out for supper. Then I have a class to teach, which I hope you will attend. Will you? You shouldn't sit here and stew."

"Of course." I had been so obsessed with my own problems I forgot completely that it was his usual night to teach. Paolo found one of my tango dresses that I kept more or less permanently at his house. It was the one he and Tanner had chosen for me when we had just met. It felt good to put it on.

"I really needed to see you in this dress," Paolo said quietly, drawing me close, "and later I will very much enjoy removing it."

We kissed, gently and sweetly, just a promise of things to come. After a light supper at a favorite local bistro, we headed to the dance studio. Cheryl and Don were pleased to see me there, and introduced me to a few new faces. Paolo's classes were growing in size, and now he had to hold them twice a week to meet the demand. He was also organizing workshops two or three times a year for the truly enthusiastic ones. Carlos and Anna showed up. They had improved tremendously since the last time I saw them dance. After the official lesson ended, Carlos and I practiced our ochos and media-lunas endlessly around the hall. Carlos did not look the least bit stressed.

It made me wonder. But I didn't dare broach the subject. I didn't want to open a conversation that could potentially annoy my employer, my client in Brazil, and the FBI. If Carlos felt no threat at work, I wasn't going to be the person to introduce one.

After the lesson we again went to the beach and walked a few miles. Paolo insisted. By the time we got home I was tired, well fed, and relaxed. Before letting Paolo remove my dress, I checked my phone for messages. Tanner had sent a photo, captioned with the name of a restaurant. The photo was a candid shot of a couple staring deeply into each other's eyes, clearly unaware that Tanner had caught them with his camera. Tsvetanka and Ben held hands across the table. I gasped, then burst out laughing.

Paolo came over to look. Tanner's message had popped the cork off of my bottled stress, and I was giggling uncontrollably. I pointed to the photo.

"Well, my goodness!" Paolo laughed, "You had better answer him."

You made my day.

We have a betting pool on the next wedding! Tanner would be the person who organized it, I'm sure.

I'll take August 15. At which time, I thought hopefully, I will not be in prison.

"Now, don't get blue," Paolo chided. "We have work to do."

I was clearly a bit upset that the day had started with a long phone call from Lourdes, which Paolo took in front of me. I think he meant to be reassuring, but it took forty-five minutes, during which they discussed every possible sequence of steps they might need to practice. Lourdes wanted him up the next weekend, and he agreed. But she clearly didn't like it when he said he would be staying with me. He was firm, but it was a struggle. I was thinking about Cygne Rouge, and wondering how well that firmness would hold up over a long weekend.

"I would have come to see you next weekend anyway," he said, looking a little irritated, "and I intend to introduce you to the lawyer I mentioned. You should go back to work on Monday, or it will look bad. Meanwhile, let's find some things out."

I have never been interested in the mysteries of the stock market. I just sock a fraction of my paycheck away in some index fund my uncle recommended, and forget about it. I never look at individual stocks or think about the financial details of anybody's business. But Paolo was looking up whatever there is to find out about King Citrus in Florida, recently gone public, and Cutrale in Brazil, privately owned and much, much larger.

"See this?" He pointed at some graphs on a brokerage web site. "This is saying that King Citrus has only two owners with controlling shares. And there are few institutional owners. I wonder who those two big owners are. I guess one of them is the former owner, who still has 20 percent of the stock, right? But who is the other one? And I wonder if the management team owns much of the stock?"

I shrugged. I couldn't see how this would make any difference to my situation. But Paolo was trying to be helpful, and I wasn't going to complain. Next we looked up everything we could find about King Citrus and its operations. Their website, which used to be nearly nonexistent, now bragged to investors about their latest equipment.

"Look, here's a mention of the new d-limonene extractor." I tried to be helpful.

"Yes. I'm noting the url and copying the full text into these notes."

"What are you hoping to find?" I really couldn't imagine why we were doing this.

Paolo looked at me oddly. "Really? You don't know why I'm doing this?" I shook my head.

"Mimi, first of all, if I don't do this, your lawyer will, at about five hundred dollars an hour. So it's worth saving the money. Second, if everything you say you talked about is already online, then it certainly can't be a trade secret, can it? Third, I'm curious where the impetus is coming from for a lawsuit. Motives for these things can be sleazy—you know, let's scare them into settling out of court and make a few easy million off of their fears. So I was wondering if King Citrus is in financial trouble."

"How would you figure that out?" I said, with a bit more interest.

"It's a publicly owned company, so they have to

make certain information available. Ah yes, see? Here is their balance sheet for last year. See? In the black for the last ten years running, nice cash flow, net profits of a couple million. Interesting. But that was all before new management, and this last year had the lowest profits of all ten years. I wonder if it is due to management bloat."

"I suppose the former owner used to get that money."

"Maybe. Or he put some of it back into the business. One thing I do know about executives is that they tend to pay themselves very well."

"Can we find that out?"

"No, not easily. But all of this will help your lawyer get started and save you in fees."

"Oh. Wow. Thank you. I would never have known to do any of this." I touched his arm, and he patted my hand reassuringly.

"Now we have to study Cutrale." And the afternoon passed in research. By the end of the day, a hundred pages of information was in Paolo's file and had been sent along to the lawyer he recommended.

Over dinner Paolo talked about his own lawsuit.

"We won forty million dollars for attempted patent infringement. We sued a major software company that tried to use our encryption algorithm without paying us. One of their employees used to be a graduate student in my department, around the time that we patented our system. He must have gotten his hands on some documentation. I think that's why they hired him in the first place. Forty million is a lot, but only a slap on the wrist for such a big company. Had we lost, however, our business would have been basically over. Instead, we now receive royalties from that same company for use of our intellectual property."

"No wonder you can live comfortably on giving tango lessons!" I laughed. "Well, good for you!"

Paolo smiled. "You know, Mimi, I never talk to anybody about the money thing. Because you never know how people will react. I keep it quiet. So please don't mention it to anybody."

"Well, it does raise questions."

"Such as?" Paolo looked at me archly.

"There's a game I play with Tammy. If you could live anywhere you wanted, where would you live? When we try to imagine such a lucky amount of resources, we get stuck. There are too many great places in the world. I would say Brazil, and Tammy would say Costa Rica. I'd say maybe the south of France, and Tammy would wonder about England. We've played at imagining this for years, but neither of us ever came up with Port Charlotte!"

Paolo laughed. "I told you why I came here—because of a girlfriend. I guess I never explained why I stayed. When our company was just starting, I had to be able to drop everything and go to Boston on a moment's notice. I did that about once every two weeks. I kept an apartment there. Thinking about a new physical place to be was just not possible in those years. Now I could move, but I'd lose my tango group. And, as you say, there are too many possibilities to consider. I find the idea of moving a bit overwhelming."

"It's a difficult game," I agreed. "But if I had a lot of money and for some reason didn't want to move, I'd sure travel a lot. I'm surprised you don't go on more adventures."

Paolo looked at me intensely. "Want to go on an adventure? I'm game. I just hate doing stuff like that by myself."

I thought about it. "Fair enough. If I were single and had a lot of money, I'd still go on adventures. I'd take Tammy."

Paolo laughed. "I bet she'd go, too," he agreed. "I really envy you your friends. For some reason, I find it hard to find close friendships like yours. I don't know why."

I thought about it. I guessed it was probably the money, which can get in the way of things sometimes. I was glad he didn't tell me about it right off. I knew he had enough money, but I hadn't realized he was rich.

"You see, now you are thinking about the money," Paolo said thoughtfully.

"Yes," I admitted. "Now I won't feel guilty about all the airfare you spend to come see me." He smiled. "But there is one thing I'm wondering about that has nothing to do with all of that."

"Oh?" Paolo went to the fridge and came back with a small piece of cheesecake and two forks.

"I danced a lot with Carlos last night. He seemed really relaxed. Why is he so relaxed if all this stuff is going down at work? It would make me completely stressed."

"Hmm," Paolo licked his spoon. "Good observation. I'll see what I can find out."

CHAPTER 7

I went back to work. I walked into Dan's office, smiled politely, and asked for something to do. Dan gave me a project to work on, figuring out specifications and costs for a new proposal to an old client, to upgrade the control system for a paper mill. As I sat down to work I realized that I had missed the problem solving and system building part of my job. I was happy when I was putting stuff together to make a factory run. It calmed me, and I stopped obsessing about King Citrus and its nonsense. Best to let the lawyer deal with them.

I finally had lunch with Tanner, who was at his nosiest. Why was Paolo in Boston without me? Why was he doing private workshops? I explained about Lourdes and the Cygne Rouge event.

"Oooh, can we party crash?" Tanner was wide-eyed at the prospect.

"No," I said firmly, "Paolo would kill us both. Besides, the location is a secret." Fortunately I hadn't said where it would be. I just pretended not to know.

"What's going on with Tsvetanka and Ben? Where did you take that picture?"

Tanner hooted. "Todd and I went out to dinner, and there they were! I don't think they saw us. At least I hope not. After all of Ben's fussing, digging his heels in and looking insulted, there he was, cooing at her. I swear, he was cooing."

"You could hear what they were saying?"

"Oh no," Tanner admitted, "but I could imagine!"

"Are Schaeffer and Lu happily married? Are you keeping an eye on them too?"

"Oh my," Tanner began, then hesitated, "I think we have to have a dinner date for me to tell you everything. So not now. In a word, yes. They are disgustingly happy."

I laughed.

"How was Brazil?" Tanner looked at me intensely.

"Weird," I admitted, "as they didn't actually seem to need me at the plant. The vacation part was great, though. Great beaches, good food, monkeys. What do you want? It's paradise."

Tanner looked at me conspiratorially.

"The FBI came around asking questions."

"Really? What about?"

Tanner leaned in to whisper. "Corporate espionage

by Cutrale. Don't be surprised if they come around. I wouldn't tell them anything if I were you."

"Why not?" I was curious to get Tanner's take on the situation, although it was way too late to get his advice.

"You never know who they might point their fingers at. For all we know they might think I'm the spy. Or you!" Tanner laughed. "Nothing seems ridiculous to them."

I laughed, a bit nervously. "I'll remember that."

After work I finally had a chance to hang out with Tammy, who was more flustered than usual.

"Nothing is more stressful than planning your wedding!" She lamented, reciting in detail the trials of pleasing both the mother and the future mother-in-law. I refrained from describing options that might be more stressful, such as the prospect of a prison sentence for discussing citrus processing with the wrong people. Instead I sympathized.

"Tell me about my dress!" I insisted.

"Maroon. Truly a bridesmaid's horror. You will hate me. And you will have to have it altered."

"That's okay," I said to console her. "It's only important that your dress is perfect. The others can be less perfect. When do I get it?"

"In about a week." Tammy looked at me. "What's not right? Your text said things were not okay. Was there a problem in Brazil? Is there something going on between you and Paolo? Tanner said he was up here without you. What's that about?"

Once again I explained about Cygne Rouge and evaded the discussion of work. Mr. Frank Stevens would have been proud of me.

"Oh, god, I'm so sorry!" Tammy seemed genuinely ashamed. "Here I am, going on about all my problems, and you sit there and listen and never whine at all about your boyfriend going off to some dance thing with another woman. Just wait 'til I see him! He'll get a piece of my mind!"

"Tammy, no," I pleaded, "it's not like that. I actually think it will be okay. We have a truce until after your wedding. He gets back just in time to escort me to it. Meanwhile, we are carrying on as usual." This didn't seem like an accurate description of the last few weeks, but it would have to do. Tammy looked at me suspiciously.

"Well, okay," she sighed. "I'll behave. But I'm not proud of him right now."

Paolo arrived for a long weekend, with a packed schedule so complicated I had him write it down for me. He seemed determined to address my situation with Cutrale directly by meeting with his lawyer, while simultaneously distracting me from the whole thing with a series of tango events, musical concerts, and social obligations. I suspect he was hoping I wouldn't notice the six hours he spent with Lourdes on Thursday, Friday, and Monday, as well as a few hours each day of the weekend. I had never experienced the competitive, perfectionist side of Paolo. I was dying to watch them practice. Barely concealed jealousy was an excellent distraction from my prospective legal hassles.

"Sweetheart," he said, hugging me gently, "before

we go to the milonga tonight, I want to teach you some new patterns. I don't want Lourdes to be the only woman I can dance these with, do you agree?" I agreed, heartily.

It had been a while since I took an actual lesson from Paolo. I was still very much a novice, with only basic steps and a few more complex maneuvers, although these had been reinforced at every dance. Paolo wanted to teach me some incredibly sexy move that included a dip with the woman's leg wrapped around the man's knee, followed by a series of tiny steps requiring much ass wiggling on my part.

"Keep both feet moving in the same line. Why are you laughing?"

"I just had no idea I could make my butt do that!"

Paolo smiled. "We'll use this move at Tammy's wedding reception, no matter what the music. Trust me, your butt will look fantastic doing this."

"Okay," I laughed. I could just imagine the look on Tanner's face. "Maybe you should teach me all your moves for Cygne Rouge."

"Oh, I'd love to, in time." Paolo kissed me gently. "Right now we have only time for a few. I'd like to do this one tonight with you, at the milonga in Newton."

After a few hours of practicing in my tiny dining room, with the furniture pushed back to its edges, we ate sandwiches and went to the dance. As usual, every woman in the room asked Paolo for a dance. Unusually, he said no to half of them, and danced with me as much as possible. Tanner and Todd arrived, unexpectedly bringing Tammy with them. I glanced at her as we glided around the room. It's great to have loyal friends, but Tammy looked particularly fierce. When we got back to our table

Paolo sailed off with another dancer, and the three of them surrounded me.

"Which one is Lourdes?" Tammy whispered.

"None of them. She isn't here tonight."

"My, my, shouldn't she be practicing?" Tanner's catty side was showing.

"Six hours Thursday, Friday, and Monday as well as earlier today and a bit tomorrow," I replied, "I expect her feet might hurt."

"Some serious stuff!" remarked Todd, adding, "Twenty hours in high heels counts as a form of torture, don't you think?"

"I certainly wouldn't know," Tanner answered, "and neither would Mimi, I suspect!"

Paolo rejoined the table. He looked around at the four of us, then smiled at Tammy.

"Am I being monitored closely?" He winked at me, and tried to look serious for Tammy, all at the same time.

"You bet!" she replied, laughing. "Somebody has to keep an eye on things for Mimi. I applied for the job a while ago, but I have to share it with Tanner now."

Paolo laughed softly. "I do envy Mimi her friends." Then he took Tammy's hand and led her, as she objected quietly, to the dance floor. Tammy got a personal tango lesson right then and there, and returned to the table looking surprised but happy.

"Wow," she said, sitting down, "maybe I was wrong. Maybe we should have tango at my wedding reception!"

"With your permission I'd like to spend a about three days investigating these businesses in more depth. I know that no charges have been brought yet, and might never be brought. But it pays to be prepared, and although my time is expensive, just three days won't be too bad." Ned Santos, Paolo's lawyer, leaned over his desk and looked me in the eye. "I can't tell without further research whether anybody could have a case against anybody here."

"Shouldn't we wait until a suit is filed?" I asked, looking at Paolo. "I don't think I did anything wrong!"

"Of course you don't," Santos replied. "That's how people get into this kind of trouble. We can wait, of course, if you like." He looked at Paolo.

"No, go ahead and start," Paolo said, looking at me reassuringly. "I think it will be money well spent."

We had just gone over everything. Santos had questioned me on every aspect of Paolo's summary report, wanting to know far more about the two processing plants than I would ever be able to tell him, as well as questioning me on any motives I could conceivably have for snitching information. Tired and stressed, we returned to my apartment to find a package had arrived. It was the dreaded maroon bridesmaid's dress. It was long and shiny, fitting loose in the bust and a little too tight in the waist. It had some goofy lace ruffles here and there and a low-cut back that would make the straps fall off of my shoulders. Paolo insisted that Todd could make it look quite good, but I was convinced that my only hope of keeping it on would be four rolls of double-sided sticky tape. We headed back out to Todd's shop and got there just a few minutes before it closed.

Todd was appropriately amused. I was fitted, refitted, and retrofitted until Todd was satisfied. The lace ruffles were delicately restrained and reduced. The low back was mysteriously made less low. The hem was raised to allow for walking or perhaps even dancing. At Paolo's request the hips were taken in so that my new wiggly tango step would be completely visible. During all of this, my phone rang repeatedly, and by the time it was over Tanner and Tammy had both arrived. Tammy was duly impressed, and Todd agreed that he would write up directions for altering the dress so that her other bridesmaids could take them to the nearest tailor.

The five of us went out for beer and pizza, celebrating the victory over the dress. At least one thing went well today, I mused, glad to be distracted from whatever legal mess lay ahead. Paolo and I smiled at each other, still lovers. Tammy observed us closely. Paolo would leave for Cygne Rouge the next evening, and I wondered if we would still be lovers when he returned. Tammy had great antennae for social and emotional things, but would she be able to tell me what was happening in Ljubljana? I didn't think so.

Paolo and I went back to my apartment. He turned his phone on and checked for messages: five from Lourdes. Could he practice tomorrow? All day? Half a day? How about tonight for an hour or two? He read them to me, shaking his head. He wrote back: enough practice, see you at the airport. As he took me in his arms the phone rang.

It was Dan with bad news. Controltech stood accused of sharing trade secrets without authorization, breaching confidentiality, and conducting industrial espionage while I was on site at Cutrale in November. It was clear now that the legal process was in motion and I could be next. Paolo emailed Santos with an injunction to go ahead full speed.

With Paolo gone there was nothing to distract me from worrying except work. I worked particularly long hours, and avoided my friends. Tammy wanted to talk about Paolo and arrive at some sort of conclusion about his behavior and choices. I needed to avoid this conversation at all costs. Tanner occasionally alluded to his chat with the FBI agent, clearly fishing for information that I wasn't going to give. Another conversation to be avoided at all costs. Todd summoned me to no less than three dress fittings, declaring this his most ambitious attempt ever to redeem a bad outfit. I went obediently but ran away at any suggestion of a social moment afterward.

"How long does it usually take to resolve these cases?" I asked Ned Santos at one of our meetings.

"Oh, it can take years sometimes," he replied, "but other times it is quite fast."

"Do you think this one will be fast?"

"Depends on what I find out. I don't want to give you false hope, Mimi. At this point it looks like they might have a case against you. Next time somebody is pumping you for information about another client, ask yourself carefully what the motives might be."

"What do you think Cutrale's motives were?"

"That is exactly what I'm trying to find out. I think I have some clues. Be patient."

Patience is not my strong suit. I was going to have to wait to find out if I might have to go to trial, or even to jail. I would have to wait and see if my lover was faithful to me, if he would still want me when he returned. Would he want me if I were in jail? He could consider lots of options at that point, but I certainly wouldn't have many. Santos jolted me out of these thoughts.

"Mimi, did anybody at King Citrus ever tell you that some process on site was private information, not to be shared?"

"No," I said, looking at him. "Does that matter?"

"It matters a lot. What exactly were you told about that d-limonene extractor?"

"That it was new, had been bought from a particular company, had not been installed yet, and therefore I didn't have to deal with its controls."

"Did you see it or work with it at all?"

"No. I just knew who made it and that it was supposed to be particularly efficient."

"Good," said Santos. "I think I see how to proceed, and I'll have something for you shortly."

"Also," I added, "my boss told me to give the customer whatever they wanted."

I felt a little bad about that statement, which clearly shifted the blame to Dan. But I knew from my conversation with him that he was all too ready to shift the blame to me.

I thanked him and left, going back to my apartment. Sitting alone and moping, unable to talk to Paolo by Skype and unwilling to risk conversation with my usual friends, I realized something. If I had to go to jail, then I had better use my remaining freedom wisely. It seemed like a good moment to attempt fun, even a sort of sad, desperate fun. And, it was the night of the milonga.

I went. I danced the night away with Tanner and Todd. For the first time ever, several men asked me to dance, and I did well with them. I mentioned this to Tanner. He smiled.

"Of course, Mimi," he explained patiently, "nobody is going to ask you to dance if Paolo wants you for a partner. He's the alpha male in this room, in case you haven't noticed. Nobody is going to walk up to his girl."

I didn't know if Tanner was right. But it was comforting to think that Paolo was the reason I never got asked to dance, rather than a general perception that I was incompetent at it. I said so.

"Believe me," said Tanner, "I have danced with every woman in this room in the last few months. You are quite good."

Tanner is a loyal friend. I wanted to believe him. For the rest of the evening, I made an effort to feel that I was "quite good." It was an exercise in self-control. I went home exhausted, had a shot of bourbon, crawled into bed and set the alarm for six. As I drifted off, the phone beeped and I opened it to a text from Paolo.

Chin up, all is and will be well.

God, I hope so.

Paolo must have been a bit worried about my state of mind. He made a real effort to set up a Skype call from Ljubljana, in spite of his all-day dance events and my determination to fend off depression with work. One early morning we connected. He was out of doors somewhere, at a hotspot in the city. He held his laptop up to give me the view—a lovely river with cafés along it, spanned by a bridge guarded by stone dragons. He asked how I was doing and I lied—*I'm okay, I'm doing fine*. I'm sure it rang false. He asked how it was going with Ned Santos, and I explained that I was waiting for his written response to the accusations leveled at me. Then I asked him how it was going.

"Well honestly, Mimi, it's fantastic. There is a reason people are dying to be asked to this event. The band is amazing, the dancers are awesome, I'm enjoying myself tremendously. Except when I'm worried about you. But frankly, I don't think you did anything wrong, so I'm taking the luxury of not being too worried. I'll be back soon, and I'll tell you all about it."

Paolo's smile faded as I heard voices in the background. As the voices got louder I could see Lourdes' face appearing in the background. She gave me an insufferably smug look and tapped Paolo on the shoulder. He said something to her I couldn't hear, and turned back to the screen.

"Got to go, sweetie. If I don't reach you before I get back, I'll see you then. Try not to worry." And he signed off before I could even say "I love you."

I took a walk to the nearest liquor store to buy a new bottle of bourbon. Spring had won its eternal battle with winter and the roses were beginning to bloom, the daffodils and tulips fading in many front yards. I thought about how nice it was to see spring, and how sad it would be to be in jail instead. I thought about all the possibilities: Paolo leaves me and I go to jail, Paolo leaves me and I don't go to jail, Paolo stays with me and I don't go to jail,

Paolo stays with me and I go to jail. Somehow the last option seemed the saddest. I made the unhappy resolution to break up with Paolo if I ended up going to jail. As long as I had to be miserable there was no point taking him with me.

Jail was just inconceivable. Here I am, puttering along day after day just doing my job and, all of a sudden, somebody thinks I deserve to be in jail. Who were these people and why did they want to do this to me? I don't have any money. Well, that's not true. I have a retirement account with about fifty thousand dollars in it. Does King Citrus need my money that badly? Or will I end up spending it all to pay Ned Santos? The options looked worse and worse the more I thought about it.

I bought my bourbon but kept on walking. A mile from my apartment I took a table at a small Italian restaurant and ordered some wine and pasta. What were my options? I needed information, but who had it? I realized that I had only one person I could trust to give me insight on my problem. I walked the mile home, relaxed from the wine and slightly consoled by the fact that, short of a solution, I at least had a plan.

"Mimi, how nice to hear from you. When will you visit again?" Carlos seemed genuinely surprised at my call.

"Carlos, I have a problem, and I hope you can help me understand some things." I proceeded to explain the entire mess, including the injunction from the FBI not to talk about it. "If you don't want to talk to me, I will understand. But I desperately need to know if I did anything wrong."

Carlos whistled. "You know what, Mimi, let me think about this and look up some stuff. I'll call you back in a bit."

I was sipping bourbon when he called back.

"You know, Mimi, that we are under new management and we went public not too long ago, right? There was an offering to employees to own some stock in the company instead of taking a cash bonus last year. So I took that offer. My bonus was never that much to begin with, and now I'm a stockholder in King Citrus. You know we get a big annual report, right? So that is what I was just reading, to see if it held any interesting information."

"Well, I know that profits were not as high this year as in previous years," I said, "but that is stuff Paolo just found on his stock trading site."

"Yes, that's right, and we are all a little worried. But here is something interesting. The former owner owns about 20 percent. The new management altogether owns about 15 percent. But 30 percent is the largest share, and it belongs to a company called Citrade Holdings. This is the largest shareholder, and they bought their stock just recently, about a month ago. I don't know if this is helpful, but maybe it will be useful to you."

I wrote it all down. "Thanks, Carlos. I don't know if it will help or not. Can I ask you one more question?"

"Of course, Mimi. But you haven't answered mine. When do you visit again?"

"I don't know. But here is my question. Do you recall if, at any point, anybody told me that certain information was private, or secret, or not to be discussed? Did anybody tell me anything like that?"

"I don't remember anybody saying that."

"Has anybody said that to you?"

"No, Mimi. Nobody has said any such thing. What do we have to hide? I can't imagine."

I thanked Carlos and got off the phone, wrote up the notes I took and emailed them to Ned Santos, praying that they would be of some use. Not long after I sent them, I got a thank you email from Santos. I was impressed.

Tammy was going nuts over the wedding. Every time she thought it was all settled, some new twist appeared to create options, decisions, arguments, and endless wasted time.

"Steve wonders why I'm a wreck," Tammy sniffed, sipping on her latte. "He just avoids all the decisions and lets me deal with two unbelievably fussy mothers. I did what you said—I put them in charge of completely different parts of the event, and still they manage to argue over everything!"

"Sounds awful," I commiserated. I'm sure it was awful, but I was so distracted by my own problems that the best I could do was pretend to sympathize. Tammy can see right through that sort of stuff.

"Look, I know you are upset about Paolo," she clucked, "but I'm pulling my hair out over this wedding."

"It will be okay," I said, patting her on the back, "Just focus on the honeymoon."

"First I have to live through the wedding. My mother chose the icky maroon colors. Now she is trying to control what Steve's mother wears. Steve's mother wants to wear a blue dress, horrors! How can we have that?" Tammy threw up her arms in mock alarm.

"Just tell them it doesn't matter as long as you are the best looking woman in the room. They will understand that."

Tammy burst out laughing. "Should I really say that?"

"I think so. Humor is the only thing that can save you now. They should get used to it, because you will probably need to use it quite often on them."

Tammy hooted.

"Consider it a training program," I continued, "in proper treatment of a daughter-in-law."

Tammy smiled. "You always cheer me up."

"Have you talked to the pastor who is doing the ceremony?"

"Oh my god, yes," Tammy laughed. "Steve and I had to answer a ton of questions, look at each other and visualize what the other one would look like at eighty, and a bunch of other stuff. I didn't dare visualize Steve at eighty, or I might have called off the wedding."

"What did you do instead?" I had to ask.

"I visualized Steve as a koala bear, which was pretty cute. The pastor had a very approving look on his face. Later, Steve told me that he visualized me as a wallaby."

"You were meant for each other," I observed.

"Exactly. We have similar coping mechanisms. I read recently that this was a definite mark of compatibility."

"Maybe you should honeymoon in Australia."

CHAPTER 8

Paolo returned in time for Tammy's rehearsal dinner, a
mere few hours to spare before the long ride to Vermont.
The scenery was spectacular: blossomy June in New
England. The church Tammy had chosen was almost
annoyingly quaint. The hotel where Paolo and I dropped
our bags was intended for the ski season, and summer
tourists wandered everywhere. A small river ran behind
the hotel, with children splashing in it. Jerome swam
through my thoughts, proof that my head was seriously
askew.

The rehearsal itself was straightforward. Evidently all
of the arguments between the mothers concerned the
reception and the dresses, leaving the ceremony up to the
happy couple. So we practiced walking in and standing
still, something I could still manage reasonably well in my
generally awful state of mind.

During the rehearsal dinner Paolo held my hand
under the table, squeezing it now and then, catching my
eye and smiling. I smiled back. Rarely have I worked so
hard not to think about anything but the present moment.

Once we were back at the hotel, things heated up immediately. Paolo didn't talk about Cygne Rouge, didn't want to hear about what the lawyer was up to or my conversation with Carlos. He just said he was so happy to see me, and set about proving it.

Tammy's wedding was another story. The two mothers sat in the front rows, one in regulation maroon and the other in vivid turquoise. Both wore corsages the size of dessert plates, in shades of pink. The bride was elegant in the flattering dress we helped her find. As she entered, Tanner and Todd quietly cheered, about five rows back. The mothers glanced disapprovingly in their direction. A slightly choppy version of "What a Wonderful World" quickly drowned out their cheers. I sincerely hoped Tanner did not know the words.

Tammy and Steve had wisely decided to keep their own words to a minimum. The pastor said the usual things, and Tammy and Steve had only to say "I do" at the appropriate moments. They were both visibly nervous, but how can you screw up "I do"? You can't. So the wedding went off without a hitch.

Before the reception we had to pose for the usual series of photos. We had a party of several women in maroon dresses, myself included, a few men in maroon suits, and the bride and groom. These photos were easy. But then the parents were included, requiring the placement of a dozen individuals in maroon, black and white, and one person in head to toe turquoise. Many opinions were afloat about how to arrange everyone. It was an arduous process in which I feared the two mothers might come to blows. Steve interceded, placing both mothers in between the bride and groom. It looked good but I feared it might foreshadow things to come. Fortunately the photographer refused, and placed them appropriately, at least in terms of family if not color palette.

A restaurant well known for its generous servings catered the reception. Friends and family tucked in to plates overloaded with chicken, steak, carrots, and three kinds of pasta salad. Evidently Steve's mother had chosen the caterer. After dinner the happy couple made a toast and cut the cake. As it was being served, Paolo excused himself and stepped outside. He returned as the traditional waltz began. A thumpy version of "Lara's theme" wafted through the reception hall as first the newlyweds, then their parents and friends, took up the dance. Paolo led me to the floor. We waltzed once around the room. The second time around, Paolo leaned in to whisper in my ear.

"I hate to break a beautiful mood, but since you don't have your cell on you, Ned texted me. He wants to see you as soon as we get back to Boston."

My stomach did a somersault. I looked at Paolo expectantly, but he just shrugged.

"That's all I know, for now. Let's not worry about it until tomorrow." Okay, I thought, I'll worry about what happened at your tango party instead.

"Actually," Paolo went on, "let's not worry about anything until tomorrow." The waltz ended and a slow romantic tune took its place. Paolo took me in a close embrace, and I let myself relax into the music. We danced every dance.

"Well, am I still your only girl?" Three days of wedding festivities, driving around New England, and eating and sleeping well had done its work. I was reasonably relaxed.

Paolo and I were still ardent lovers, and he even brought me coffee in bed. Now it was time to deal with matters.

Paolo smiled. "If you will still have me," he replied graciously. Alas for Paolo, I've had my share of insincere boyfriends.

"So, did anything happen between you and Lourdes?"

Paolo gave me a reassuring hug. "Only on the dance floor," he said, smiling. "And even then, I was thinking of you."

I gave a sigh of relief.

"So that is one worry you don't have any more, okay? Let that go."

"What if they invite you next year?"

"Well, if they invite me, you will be my partner."

"And if they invite Lourdes?"

Paolo did not reply immediately. He acted as if this possibility had not occurred to him until now. I found that hard to believe.

"Well, I hadn't really considered that," he answered, "but to me it seems unlikely that Lourdes would want me to be her partner a second time."

"Why would you think such a thing!" I couldn't believe anybody would miss a chance at a tango weekend with Paolo.

"Let's put it this way. She didn't get everything she wanted from me." He looked up at me and smiled archly. "So, she flirted madly with every other guy on the dance floor." Paolo watched my reaction closely. I giggled.

"So," he continued, "she pissed off several women by flirting with their partners, boyfriends, husbands, whatever. It will be a miracle if she is invited back to Cygne Rouge. Some of those people must be in charge! However, she may have caught the eye of one fellow, a wonderful dancer from Berlin. In the event he is invited next time, perhaps she can go as his partner."

I was grinning happily at this point. Paolo laughed. "So you see that things do work out!" he admonished.

"Karma," I replied.

"Maybe," he agreed. "Speaking of which, you need to call work and tell them you won't be there today."

"Why is that?" I was doing my best to keep up appearances at work, although the stress of the King Citrus accusations was making it hard to do so.

"Because we are going to see Ned. I promised him I'd have you at his office first thing."

"Well, we are at an interesting impasse," Ned looked at me sternly.

"How so?" Paolo inquired on my behalf. Just being in the lawyer's office made me so nervous that I found it hard to speak.

"The good news is that, in my opinion, they do not have a case against you." I breathed an audible sigh. Ned smiled at me and Paolo gave me a hug.

"It appears," he went on, "that all of the technical

information you gave to Cutrale was actually available in the annual report that was published just after you returned from Brazil. It is possible to obtain this report electronically because, as you know, King Citrus is now a publicly owned company. Their annual report is available to stockholders, of which I am now one. So, in effect, it is a cheaply available to anybody who wants it."

"Sounds like Mimi is off the hook," agreed Paolo.

"Alas, King Citrus may not see it that way. You see, Mimi went to Cutrale before all of this information was public. Some of it was on the King Citrus web site. In particular, the web site did mention the purchase of the d-limonene extractor, but without mentioning the manufacturer. King Citrus could insist that the timing of their release of information was important and that Mimi should not have shared that information in advance of its public announcement."

"I never told them the name of the manufacturer!" I was pretty sure about that, since I couldn't remember it myself.

"Are you absolutely sure about that?" Ned stared intently at me.

"Well, no, because my memory is not perfect."

"But you are mostly sure."

"Yes."

"What is the name of the manufacturer?"

"Extenda, I think," I replied, remembering that I gave the name to Frank Stephens from the FBI.

"So you could swear in court that you did not

remember the name of the manufacturer nor do you remember sharing that information with anyone?"

"No," and I explained that I had given the name to Stephens.

"Ned," Paolo interrupted, "something is really bothering me about this whole thing. It just sounds like there is no case. Why, then, would King Citrus go forward with one, when such cases are so expensive?"

Ned Santos rocked back in his chair. He took a small bronze figurine of a bull off a nearby shelf, and turned it over and over in his hands.

"I can't say for certain," he replied, "but I have some guesses. As your friend Carlos pointed out, the company did not do as well last year as in some previous years. It's not such a big operation, but it was in the red for a few million dollars. Needless to say, that is not a good thing at the moment when a business goes public. They had trouble with the I.P.O. and the stock price has fallen a bit since then. I suspect they are hoping to settle out of court and get a few million to balance the books."

"I don't have a few million!" I was gasping at the thought, "or even any sizeable fraction of a million!"

"But Controltech does," Ned pointed out, "and if you agree to settle out of court for even a hundred thousand, Controltech will look like it shares some of the responsibility."

"Mimi," Paolo said, "you are the first domino."

"Does Controltech even have that kind of money?" I found it hard to imagine.

"Of course," Ned replied. "I've looked into that

also. I believe they have some considerable funds. It's impossible to know exactly how much, as they are not publicly owned and their records are private. But given the number of employees they have, it is likely that they keep at least five million in reserve. Think about all the paychecks and expense reimbursements they do each month. And consider that their customers do not always pay on time. From my experience with other companies, I would expect them to have at least that much on hand."

My head was swimming. It was hard to imagine why King Citrus would do this to me, after all the years I had been going there, fixing their systems, drying wires out with a hairdryer, listening to endless swearing. The top management of the last year I never met though, and I supposed they didn't care much about me, or my work there.

"A penny for your thoughts," Paolo gently put his arm around me.

"Well," I said, "if it's just about money, should we just give up and pay it? Although I don't have much socked away, and I'd have to start from scratch to build up my savings and retirement accounts again."

"It's not that simple," Ned said flatly, fingering the little bull. "If you settle out of court it amounts to admitting guilt. Controltech will not want you back. If they settle out of court it will not help their business either. You will be broke and out of a job. Controltech will take a hit and probably survive, but it won't help your situation one bit."

"So then we have to go to court?" I wasn't thrilled by the prospect in the least.

"That depends"—Ned held the small bull and stared

out the window—"on the FBI and federal prosecutors. King Citrus will not press charges directly through a private lawyer. The FBI does the investigation and a U.S. attorney from the Economic Crimes Unit will prosecute. My job is to convince them there is no case to be brought in the first place."

"Then it's over?" I asked, hoping for a yes.

"Yes, then it's over." Ned glanced at me. "But we can't count on it. If they do bring charges, my job then becomes to prove your innocence. I am close to being able to do this. Close."

"If you can do that, then why would they bring charges in the first place?"

Ned looked at me. "Because at the moment I am not ready. There are a few things I still cannot explain. Why did Cutrale ask you so many questions? I understand, more or less, why you answered their questions. You thought the information was unimportant, was well known, was just chit-chat. But why did they ask in the first place? I need more time, and a way to get some information from Cutrale. Second, how secret was the new d-limonene extractor? I need a way to get some information about that also."

"Have you talked to Carlos?" I could tell from Ned's expression that I had not mentioned this before. "Here, I'll give you his phone number. He gave me all of the information about who owned shares in King Citrus, which I gave to you. He works there. Please though, don't get him in trouble. He is a good friend."

Ned took the phone number down in his notes. "I'll give him a call tomorrow," he promised. "Do you have any contacts at Cutrale?"

I thought about that and got out my phone. There were a couple of Brazilian numbers on it, and I tried to remember whose they were. I identified numbers for Alberto, the engineer, and Claudio, his boss. Ned took these down also.

"Mimi, this is good," he said encouragingly, "but I must warn you that if Cutrale were indeed trying to get private information out of you, they will probably not be helpful to us. If, on the other hand, there was a good reason to ask you these questions, then they might be of use. I'll let you know how it turns out. It will probably take me a few weeks to make sense of whatever they, and Carlos, say."

Paolo and I looked at each other.

"Can we ask for more time to prepare?" To me, this just seemed reasonable. Paolo looked at me sadly.

"Unfortunately, you can only ask for such time after charges are brought." Paolo's expression was serious. Looking at Ned, he asked, "Do you have any idea when that would be?"

"No, that is entirely up to the FBI." Ned set the bull squarely between us. "Which brings me to my next point."

Paolo got up abruptly and went to the window, staring out of it.

"If the feds press charges, I will advise you whether to settle out of court, plead innocent, or plead guilty. My advice will depend on what I discover in the next few weeks. Right now, I'd say plead innocent. But that recommendation may change with further information."

"Okay," I agreed. "You will let me know when they press charges?"

"No, Mimi. You will let me know."

"Won't they talk to you directly? As in, see my lawyer?"

"No, Mimi. This would be a federal case."

"They'll bring me papers?"

Ned stared at the little bull. "No, my dear. They will arrest you."

When Paolo started to come to work with me, only Dan wasn't surprised. Gallantly refusing to leave me alone, lest I be arrested without suitable company, he accompanied me everywhere from the moment we left Ned Santos's office. I went to work to save appearances. I wore nicer clothes than usual in case I was arrested. In reality I was useless, endlessly distracted by my thoughts and jumping at every knock on the partially open office door.

Tanner took this to mean that Paolo and I were on the superhighway to matrimony. Unable to suppress himself, he teased me endlessly with various innuendos. At one point I was eating my lunch at the computer, Paolo reading in a nearby chair, when I heard raised voices a few doors down, in the lunchroom. Dan, never given to outbursts, was loudly telling Tanner to mind his own business. A moment later there was a knock on my door. I jumped.

"Mimi," said Dan gently, "may I have a word with you?"

"Of course," I smiled.

"Privately?" he glanced at Paolo.

"No," said Paolo firmly. Dan sighed.

"Fine." Dan pulled up a chair and sat down. "Mimi, I feel we should talk about what is happening with King Citrus. I know you didn't use the lawyer I suggested. I hope you are talking to somebody though. It's great to have the support of friends," and here he glanced at Paolo, "but you do need a professional."

"I have a lawyer," I said flatly. Dan raised his eyebrows.

"Good," he said, looking at me, then away. "Well, I just wanted to be sure." He glanced again at Paolo. "Tell me, Mimi, do you think you gave away any trade secrets to Cutrale?"

I was caught off guard. Paolo looked over in alarm and shook his head. No cards were to be shown.

"That depends," I stalled.

"On what?" Dan said in alarm.

"On what you consider a trade secret." At this, Paolo nodded slightly. I decided that a good offense was in order, before the next question came. "Are you expecting the feds can win the case against Controltech?"

Dan sputtered. "It depends!" He threw his hands up in the air.

"On what?" I asked gently.

Dan stared at me, his face reddening. I suspect that, until that point, he believed I was unaware of the

implications that my decisions would have for
Controltech.

"On you!" He rose quickly from his chair, glared at
Paolo, and left, slamming the door behind him. For a
moment we breathed in the silence.

"Ned suspected. Now we know." Paolo handed me
my purse. "Let's take a little walk and make a few phone
calls, shall we?"

"Frank Stevens be damned." Paolo had made up his mind
to out me. Tammy and Steve were back from their
honeymoon and eager to tell me all about it. Tanner and
Todd wanted to try out a new restaurant specializing in
medieval Sephardic dishes. I was into any gourmet-meal-
in-my-best-dress kind of event, in case it should be my
last for a while. Paolo had scouted the restaurant and
asked for a table in a private room in the back. I could
now see why he did this.

"And who is that?" Tammy paused in her
description of the budget resort in Antigua where she and
Steve had spent their honeymoon, returning with
matching sunburns.

"Oh dear," said Tanner, "I was afraid there were
things you weren't telling me. Does this have anything to
do with Paolo's charming presence at work every day?" I
nodded silently.

Paolo gave a full-length version of my sorry
situation. Tammy stared in amazement while I ate my
lovely dish of lamb with nuts and honey, pretending to be
calm. I made a point of chewing each mouthful slowly,
savoring the tastes of honey and cinnamon against the
salty lamb. For weeks now I had been focusing on little

details of life, in the hope that concentrating on sensory pleasures would keep my sanity within reach. It had, more or less, worked.

"One nasty thing," Paolo went on, "is that the FBI always asks people to be cooperative and talk to no one. Then, when they indict the person, they show up with handcuffs and issue a press release—sometimes, at any rate. Thank you for being cooperative."

"I tried to get you to talk to me," Tanner said reproachfully, "but you were such a good girl, and didn't."

"Actually, the only way Mimi can defend herself is by talking. Not only to her lawyer, but also to the people she worked with in both places, via her lawyer," Paolo pointed out, "but it is true that the talking is better done by the lawyer. In that respect, the FBI has offered helpful advice."

"So, the whole time you were at our wedding, laughing and joking and being the best friend ever, you were waiting to be arrested?" Tammy had stopped eating entirely and her eyes filled with tears.

"Not exactly," I laughed, "because at that point I didn't realize they might just show up at any moment. I guarantee that would have taken most of the fun out of the day." I sipped the expensive zinfandel Paolo had ordered, and rolled it around in my mouth. Maybe there is a way to get a bottle of wine in jail. Paolo would have to buy it for me, after King Citrus takes all my life savings. I tried not to think about it. Day after day, I was putting a lot of energy into not thinking about the biggest problem in my life. I wouldn't call it denial, I'd call it self-defense.

Paolo's cell rang. He took the call in front of the group. "Yes," he said, "yes, by all means do that. Consider it covered." He hung up and looked at me. "Ned has a colleague in São Paolo who will do some local work there. Perhaps Cutrale will have some useful information for us after all."

Tammy caught my eye. I'll pay him back. I mouthed the words to her. She smiled, and a tear dropped. I suspected she found the whole thing romantic. I chewed on a garlicky artichoke that had been sautéed in very good olive oil, and followed it with some crunchy fresh bread, trying to think about how nice it is to have bread with a really good crust on it.

Tanner took out his phone, and searched it for something. When he found it, he sent it directly to Paolo.

"What is this?" Paolo asked. "Whose phone number is this?"

"That would be the factory foreman at King Citrus. If Mimi got any private information, it would have been from him. And he would be just a guilty as anybody else for giving it out."

"Ah! Excellent," and Paolo immediately composed a message for Ned, giving him the number.

"Hey, wait!" I protested, "That guy is a total loose cannon. Who knows what he'll do if Ned tells him what's going on!"

"I'll pass that along," said Paolo, smiling.

"Well, we have to make sure you aren't in the hoosegow for the next wedding!" Todd winked at Tanner.

"Wait, what? Are you two getting married?" I was sure Tanner would have said something to me about it.

Tanner leered at Todd, who coughed and looked at his plate.

"Not at the moment," said Tanner, laughing. "But Ben and Tsvetanka have something in the works. I'm just sure of it."

"No way!" I smiled. "Impossible. It's too soon. And I disapprove! And you are the worst gossip ever."

"Quite likely," agreed Todd affably.

Tanner *is* the worst gossip ever. As a result I had to endure two of the longest weeks in my life. At work every single person looked upon me with pity. People dropped in with cookies. Schaeffer offered to pick up lunch sandwiches for both Paolo and me, at least five times. Ben actually came by with a flower. There has never been a flower in any office at Controltech. It was a first. With one exception, nobody said anything specific about the situation—we are engineers, after all.

Ljudmila came into my office and cried. She couldn't believe I would do anything dishonest. She couldn't believe how evil the Cutrale executives must be. I assured her that they didn't seem evil at all. She couldn't believe that King Citrus would press charges against somebody who had been there year after year. She wanted details and I refused to give them. I just joked with her and said she could drop by the jail any time with a decent meal if she liked. By the time she got out of my office I was shaking with stress. Paolo, witnessing the entire performance, almost managed to suppress a laughing fit when she left. It was infectious, luckily.

At the end of two weeks, around three in the afternoon, Dan came by the office.

"It's time to have a serious talk," he said, "about the general situation here at work."

"Okay," I agreed, "the stress levels here are pretty high at the moment."

"I've done my best to shield my employees from the King Citrus drama."

"Yes," I said, "by keeping them ignorant. Which was probably a good idea."

"And then you told everybody about it. And now no work is getting done."

"She told nobody," Paolo interceded, "I did. I told only one person about Mimi's situation, and I did not mention the lawsuit being brought against Controltech."

"Who?" demanded Dan.

"And that person chose to share the information with everyone, which is their prerogative."

"I can't have this in my company!" Dan was truly upset and angry.

"But, you can't keep it secret forever," I argued, "because Controltech is also be in trouble. In at least as much trouble as I am."

Dan looked at me, his eyes narrowing.

"I think you should take a leave of absence," he insisted, almost shouting.

"For how long?" I asked. "And with pay?"

"Leave on your own charges and your own dime. Come back when invited. Case closed." Dan turned to leave my office, but Paolo blocked the door.

"Please, Dan," Paolo said quietly, finger raised in admonition. "Please notice that everyone is talking about the problems Mimi is having. Nobody is talking about the problems your company may well have shortly. Nobody is looking at you with pity or bringing you flowers like it's a funeral. But if you fire Mimi, next week people will know all about the implications of her situation for Controltech. You might get cookies. Or you might lose other employees too. Because they will see how much their own loyalty is valued. And I assure you, Mimi will have said nothing."

Dan sat back down.

"I just wish you had followed my advice about the lawyer," Dan said sadly, "and perhaps all of this could have been avoided. Our lawyer says the case is very weak."

"But the FBI is not yet convinced," Paolo pointed out.

"If Mimi were just to admit that she accidentally leaked some information, we could probably just settle out of court." Despair filled Dan's words.

"And for every dollar they got out of Mimi, they would get a hundred out of Controltech." Paolo said these words gently, but they were not gentle words.

"Why do you say that? We didn't do anything wrong!"

"Neither did Mimi. But Controltech is much, much richer than Mimi. And it authorized her to do what she did."

"When did I do that?" Dan shouted defensively. The veins stood out on his forehead and his face reddened. I could see that this business was taking a huge toll on him also. I wanted to have sympathy, but couldn't.

"Just give the customer whatever they want," I said, waving my hand dismissively.

It was a blessed relief not to be at work, and also a relief to get paid. Dan had eagerly relented on that point. But what do you do with yourself while you're waiting to see if you will be arrested? Paolo distracted me with hours of intensive tango lessons, day trips here and there, and long hikes. Tammy, on the other hand, took me shopping, with Paolo tagging along.

And what do you buy if you think you might go to jail? I bought stuff for my mother and my two sisters, who all live very far away. And we discussed the issue of how to tell them I was in jail, if that came to pass.

There was a famous case of a process control engineer at a razor company who sold secrets to the competitors. He did it on purpose, and probably cost that company millions. He owed a million himself, after pleading guilty, and spent over two years in jail. I looked up his case, and every other case like it. Tammy and Paolo and I discussed whether it would be possible to conceal the fact that I was in jail from my mother and sisters, for a year or two. Maybe I could just get out, go visit them, and claim it had been really busy at work. They don't see me much anyway. It might work.

I was trying on a light blue loose weave linen sweater that I thought my mom might like. Tammy chose various accessories and made me add them to the outfit. A navy scarf with yellow lilies looked pretty good, and some huge bangles made out of plastic wrapped tightly in braided electrical tape added a certain edge to the ensemble. I couldn't imagine my mother wearing electrical tape in any decorative capacity. Maybe in an invisible location, say if her underwear tore.

"Do you think your mom will be surprised to get a bunch of presents in the mail?" Tammy was scouring the racks for a skirt that would complete the outfit. "What size does she wear?"

"She's one size bigger than me," I replied, "and she'll be astonished to get a random present. I can usually barely manage a birthday card, and her birthday is months off. Well, at least I'll get some thank you notes, and the post office can forward them." Tammy smiled wryly.

"I think it's more likely that you will be a free woman sitting on your own sofa when your mom returns the favor and mails you some clothes that she has picked out. I hope you like them!"

I laughed. It took years of training to get my mom and sisters to stop sending me clothes. For a while I kept what they sent me. I could impersonate a bank teller, a club kid, or a mom-on-the-go at will. I am none of these things. I wore the bank teller outfit to Tammy's cousin's baby shower. I was overdressed. I wore the club kid outfit on a date, which turned out to be miniature golf. The high heels and the short dress made it nearly impossible to bend over enough to hit the ball. The mom-on-the-go had such cheerful colors I couldn't put it on at all.

"If I'm in jail then at least I won't feel obliged to wear them," I joked.

The saleslady looked up from the pile of clothes she

was tagging, disapproval all over her face. Tammy was pulling a knee-length white skirt from the rack.

"Try this on with it and we'll see if it might work for your mom." I obediently went into the dressing room and put on the entire outfit. I came out and modeled for Tammy. Paolo laughed.

"I feel I'm looking into the future," he chuckled, "at what you might be wearing during a happy retirement."

I looked at myself in the mirror. My own baleful expression startled me. No wonder the guys at work had been bringing me sandwiches at lunch. Now that everybody knew my troubles, I let myself stop hiding my general unhappiness.

"Can I bring you a different size?" asked the saleslady. She was polite, but pursed her lips like a child sucking a lemon.

"Um, no," I said, somewhat apologetically, "these are for my mom."

"Yes, I heard you say that," she replied curtly, "but you might get a better idea of how they look if you put on your own size."

"Ah!" interjected Paolo, "I have an idea. Let Tammy try them on for you. I guarantee they will look more cheerful on her." The saleslady looked at him oddly. Tammy and I went back into the dressing room and she put on the outfit. We both came out and I looked on while she studied herself in the mirror.

"These are nice," Tammy said guardedly, "but they do have that over-sixty vibe." The saleslady, clearly over sixty, rolled her eyes. I looked her in the eye.

"Would you wear this?" I asked. She looked at me coldly. "No, I'm serious. My mom is about your age, and she dresses a bit like you. I wonder if you would wear this outfit this way."

Taken off guard, the woman raised her eyebrows and came closer for a clear look.

"I guess not," she admitted, "I'd wear the top and scarf with jeans."

"How would you wear the skirt?" I wondered if she ever would wear it. She looked thoughtful.

"A navy top, maybe with dots."

"Thank you," I offered. She looked at me a little bit more softly now.

"It's nice of you to buy a whole outfit for your mom, but maybe you should just go with the sweater and scarf. No need to overdo it. My daughters sometimes give me stuff and I wonder just how old they think I am!" She smiled.

"Good point," I agreed, "and since I might not see her for a while, that's not the reaction I want her to have." A tear rolled disobediently down my cheek. The saleslady looked alarmed.

"There, there, dear," she cooed, "You're not really going to jail, are you?"

"We certainly hope not, dear lady," Paolo replied. "And she certainly doesn't deserve it. However the forces of the legal system do not always get the right answer."

"My goodness, and I certainly don't mean to be nosy," she began, pausing briefly when Tammy snorted, "but who did you cross?"

"An orange juice factory," I replied honestly, "in South Florida."

I bought the sweater and scarf, and we moved on to the next store. It always surprises me how strangers react to random bits of information. First the saleslady looked at me like I was a criminal, then she became my best friend when I compared her to my mother. People can come to so many conclusions from so little data. Take King Citrus, for example. They had absolutely no data that Cutrale knew anything about their operation, at least as far as I knew.

Tammy and I were discussing this at length while I tried on some pants I thought my mom might like, when my phone rang. I didn't get to it in time. Before I could retrieve it from my purse, which Paolo was holding, his phone rang and he answered it.

"She is trying on clothes that she might buy for her mother, since she is not sure what her immediate future holds. How has it gone?" I could tell by Paolo's tone that he had Ned Santos on the line. "Sure, we can come by. Is it okay if Mimi's friend comes also?"

So I didn't buy my mother the pants after all, and the three of us headed downtown to Ned's office. He greeted us warmly and brought in an extra chair for Tammy. The little bull was on the desk. Ned picked it up.

"You know, the bull in a bullfight is an innocent creature," he mused aloud, "and no matter how well it fights, it still gets killed in the end, at least in the Spanish tradition. However, there are other traditions, like the French and the Portuguese, who respect the bull and spare him. I keep this little statue to remind me of this. The bull is innocent, and yet there could be many different endings to his story, depending on the culture in which the story happens."

Paolo looked worried, and I fidgeted. Tammy just seemed confused.

"Mimi," he went on, "thanks to your colleagues in Brazil, and my colleague in Brazil, and rather a lot of chopp, the situation has become much clearer."

"Do tell," Paolo said encouragingly.

"Do you remember Carlos telling us about the stockholders? And in particular, an entity called Citrade Holdings that bought a controlling share of King Citrus stock? This was a mysterious private company. I could find little information about it. Fortunately I convinced Frank Stevens that it was important enough to investigate. They discovered that it was foreign owned, out of Andorra, which basically means nothing."

"How unhelpful. But it was nice of them to check." Paolo was making chit-chat, to get Ned to the point.

"Not completely unhelpful. It turns out that one of the owners of Cutrale is from Andorra. Which, by the way, is the money laundering capital of the planet. My Brazilian colleague used some of these facts as a starting point in his conversation with Claudio, who told him that Cutrale was expanding its reach into foreign markets and found it convenient, for, ahem, tax purposes, to use an Andorran account."

"Wow," I commented. I had no idea orange juice production could be part of such intrigue.

"Claudio claimed the whole thing was completely

above board, and merely a matter of managing too many forms of currency. Currency conversions are Andorra's bread and butter. So Cutrale banks there when conducting foreign investments. To avoid confusion, it created a spinoff company to handle foreign investments, which it named Citrade Holdings."

"What?" I laughed aloud, "Cutrale actually bought King Citrus? After what I told them?"

"No, because of what you told them. In fact, they brought you there to pump you about King Citrus before they made the decision to buy. Whatever you said must have been reasonably positive, because they bought just enough stock to control the company. You should have seen Frank Stevens face when I told him that."

"You mean the FBI couldn't figure this out, but you did?"

"As I said," and here Ned winked, "it took a lot of chopp. And we were lucky I had an old buddy, same Dartmouth class as me, who happened to be a smart lawyer in the right place at the right time."

"And so?" Paolo pressed.

"And so no charges will be brought against Ms. Darrow, and the charges against Controltech will be dropped. The statement to that effect arrived this morning and I have it here." Ned showed me the legal papers. I didn't actually read them. I was too relieved to care.

"Anything else?" Paolo asked with a smile.

"Well, yes," replied Ned, smiling back. "Since the executives at Cutrale were made aware of the actions of the King Citrus management, a few other things have happened. In particular, those managers aren't there anymore. A few Brazilians have been installed in their places. Don't be surprised if they call you, Mimi. They might need your help figuring out how to run the place. At least, Carlos tells them they need it."

Dan called in the morning and we congratulated each other on our happy ending. But I said I could use a few more weeks off, at no pay if necessary. He agreed to this, and mentioned that he might take some time off himself, with Ben in charge in his absence. He kindly suggested we might both get paid, in the spirit of recuperation after an on-the-job injury. But first, he insisted, there would be a celebratory party for everyone at Controltech, as by now everybody knew that not only me but also the company was the target of a major lawsuit. People understood that their jobs were at stake, thanks to the tireless communication of Tanner.

Controltech usually has exactly one party per year, at exactly the same time of year, in exactly the same place. The food is always the same, and the same extended family members are in attendance. It's a pleasant but predictable affair. This party was the most spontaneous social event Controltech had ever seen. We gathered after work at a local restaurant with a decent bar. Dan picked up the tab for several rounds of drinks. Only a few spouses and partners came along, but these included Todd, Paolo, and Tsvetanka. Most of the guys didn't want their wives to understand how close they had potentially come to unemployment.

After the first drink, Dan gave a short speech, lying convincingly about his appreciation for and dedication to Controltech's loyal employees. He toasted me for handling the situation well, and announced that we would both be taking time off over the next two weeks.

After the second drink, Tanner decided to give a speech. Dan cringed visibly. Tanner proceeded to describe his arrival in Florida, and his surprise at my announcement that I was seeing my tango instructor. He talked about the swearing plant manager, the sexist managers that thought an extra "man" was needed to do a simple job, the nasty repairs I had done on a rat-infested mess of wires. He talked about how much he liked Paolo. There were giggles.

"Not that way," he reprimanded, "you all just have dirty minds."

At this point even Dan was laughing.

Then he talked about my frustration with Cutrale, where they didn't seem to need my help at all. He thanked Paolo for finding a top lawyer to deal with my situation. And then he thanked me for being his best friend. By the end of his speech, I was crying. A cheer went up from the crowd, and I was toasted a second time.

"Would you like to say a few words?" Paolo whispered in my ear.

"Oh my god, no thanks," I replied.

The whole group adjourned to a back room for dinner. Ljudmila and Schaeffer joined the table with Paolo, Tanner, Todd, and me. Ljudmila looked like she had been crying for hours.

"I was so worried about you, Mimi, and I didn't even realize that all of our jobs were at stake. You are my hero," she exclaimed sincerely. Schaeffer looked slightly jealous. Ljudmila looked at him sternly. "She saved your job, too."

Schaeffer patted her hand. "I'm just glad it's over." Turning to me, he added, "The household has been quite tense for the last few weeks. Nothing like having both wage earners in the same leaky boat."

I smiled. Schaeffer had molded himself perfectly into the role of patriarch of a multi-generation household. I suspected, not for the first time, that he didn't understand whom he had married.

Dinner arrived, a lavish spread of Asian dishes. Some were outrageously spicy and others sweet and cooling. Small hills of rice dotted the tables. I ate slowly, savoring the malty overtones of some of the sauces. I sipped a Thai iced tea and let the sweetness hit me like a cold breeze. I smiled at Paolo.

"We could come here again next week," I said, "because I won't be in jail!"

Paolo put his arm around my shoulder. "And I am as happy about that as you are," he gently replied.

A few tables over, people began clinking their glasses. Worried that they would make me say something, I could feel my pulse race. When the talking quieted down, however, Ben stood up.

"I feel that there is more to be said about Mimi's year. I think we should also recognize the valuable mentor that she has been to our new colleague Ljudmila."

"Yes!" Ljudmila exclaimed, and instigated a round of applause.

"I, of all people, am grateful for our new hire." At this, people chuckled nervously. Everybody knew by now that Ben was seriously dating Tsvetanka. And of course they remembered how firmly he objected to hiring Ljudmila.

"And so I propose a toast to three lovely ladies, Mimi, Ljudmila, and her charming sister Tsvetanka!" And so we were toasted by the toasted, a room full of slightly bleary-eyed, chili pepper stuffed, massively relieved engineers. Ben cleared his throat to indicate he was not quite done.

"And I am pleased to announce the coming wedding of Miss Tsvetanka Dineva to yours truly, the undeserving Ben." There was a moment of stunned silence, and then we engineers clapped and cheered until the restaurant management came in to ask us to quiet down.

"You just can't ask more from a party than that," Tanner observed as we left. Paolo laughed.

"I told you, you are under siege. Let's see how many more relatives desire citizenship."

"Such a cynic!" Tanner reproached.

"None of them had better be interested in you," Todd said sternly.

"I doubt Ljudmila has a gay Bulgarian cousin," Tanner replied.

"You never know," said Paolo ominously, "but you will shortly."

"You are all awful. I say good luck to Ben." I pulled Paolo in the direction of the subway, and we headed home to plan a desperately needed vacation.

Paolo and I drove to a woodsy corner of New Hampshire and rented a cabin on a lake. We rented kayaks and paddled all day some days. Other days we took walks and swam. Motorboats putted by slowly, fishing poles hanging over the sides. We grilled steaks and drank wine with dinner. The other campers were surprised when we took our boombox out on the beach after dark and danced in the sand. I could almost hear them whispering to each other: these people are in love.

It was a few days before Paolo broke the news to me about Ned Santos's bill. It would eat my entire retirement fund. But so be it. This was a huge improvement on being in jail. I said so to Paolo, and thanked him once again for getting Ned on my side. Paolo looked at me quizzically.

"You don't think I'd let you lose your entire retirement fund, do you?"

"What do you mean? I'm not a criminal sitting in jail. That's what counts!"

"You are absolutely right," Paolo smiled, "but I don't want you to be broke either."

I looked at him.

"So I paid it," he said flatly, his hand on my shoulder.

"But, you didn't have to do that!" I stupidly protested. He just smiled.

"Do you think you will go back to Controltech?" Paolo asked. "And tell me, do you want to?"

It's true that, when I really thought about going back

to the office, my stomach turned upside down. All those people would look at me differently. I wondered if Dan would treat me better, worse, or the same. I had naively trusted everyone at work, but now I felt a bit differently about Dan.

"You know, I just don't know."

"Well, it's up to you of course. But I didn't want you to go back because you had to rebuild your savings."

"Thank you. My God, thank you. I suppose I could look for a different job. But I hate looking for jobs."

Paolo shook his head slowly, smiling.

"Mimi, there's a week-long tango workshop next month in Buenos Aires. Want to go? As my guest, of course."

This, I said to myself, is a quiz.

I'm not the kind of person who gives up a career entirely to become a tango bum, much as I love to dance. Dan and I reached an agreement. I would work half time and Controltech would continue to provide benefits. Paolo and I would take advantage of opportunities as they came along, which they did with increasing frequency. Cutrale contacted Controltech and arranged for me to be the process control supervisor for all their non-Brazilian holdings, which at present consisted only of King Citrus and one other processing plant in Sicily. Nobody at work felt the least bit sorry for me.

"I could do this forever," I remarked to Paolo. "It's really amazing how little money you actually need."

"Mmm," he agreed. "You seem very balanced right now. Tell me, do you have any hidden urges? Like for a trip to Brazil?"

"How about Ljubjana?" I teased. "But seriously, I do get wanderlust now and then. I think the current work situation allows room for that, don't you?"

"Certainly," he said, smiling. I have a lot of ideas about cool stuff to do, if you will come with me."

"I'll do my best," I said encouragingly.

"I have a few places in mind," he ventured.

"Yes to everything," I said, laughing. "Just give me the calendar. And I'll give it to Dan. Leave space for an annual trip to Sicily."

"Will do," he agreed.

We spent the evening looking at each other's dream destinations. It's far better foreplay than a movie, especially if you really mean it. I realized that I didn't know Paolo as well as I thought. Yes, he was obsessed with tango, but he wasn't above a camping trip or a whitewater raft adventure. His bucket list tended to be full of interesting cities. If we did everything we both wanted, we would have to live another hundred years.

I stared at Paolo and tried to imagine what he would look like in thirty years.

"Is something wrong?"

I kissed him gently. "Not at all," I smiled, leading him to the bedroom.

Sometime in the month of August, Paolo and I were enjoying a milonga in Buenos Aires.

We came down for a workshop that Paolo wanted to attend. I, of course, attended as well. I was afraid that I would be the outlier, with less experience and far less talent than the hotshots who came from around the world. Fortunately, Paolo was the perfect partner.

"Just follow my lead and relax," he said gently, as we tried some new moves and the instructor came by now and then to correct us.

Several of those at the workshop were acquaintances of Paolo. He quietly pointed a few out: this one was at Cygne Rouge; that one went last year.

At the end of a long day of lessons came the milonga, a chance to try our new steps and watch some of the best dancers in Argentina show off their moves. When one of the famous dancers stepped forward, everyone else sat down and watched. The couple had the entire floor to use, unencumbered by other dancers. The effect was amazing, an intimate dialogue translated into a public display. I watched the man closely. I suppose I should have been watching his partner, taking a lesson from her. But I watched him instead. He was focused on her body, gently steering it around the room and inviting her into complicated patterns. He looked like he was trying to be sure she was having a good time. He held her so close that I wondered how she could breathe.

It was time for everyone else to dance. The music was a flowing, vibrant tune. Paolo looked as handsome to me as ever. I was relaxed and slightly elated. The tune was called "Sweet Vertigo," a perfect description of my state of mind at that moment. As the music ended, Paolo gave me a sweet kiss on the cheek, reminding me of that first kiss goodnight in Port Charlotte. It was my turn to ask a question.

"A penny for your thoughts," I whispered.

Paolo turned silently and led me into a small garden outside.

"You are my favorite dance partner," he whispered.

"And you are mine," I returned.

"Will you go with me to Cygne Rouge next time it happens?"

"You wouldn't be embarrassed? I'm still feeling like such a beginner."

"No, I won't be embarrassed, because we will go to several more of these workshops, and we will practice. You will be spectacular."

"Do you think they will invite you?"

"Yes."

"Let me think about it. I don't want to hold you back."

There, in the moonlight, he took me in his arms and kissed me. One hand slid into his pocket and pulled out a small box. In a moment he had slipped something onto my finger, still holding me tight.

"Please say yes," he murmured.

ABOUT THE AUTHOR

After a decade as a professional engineer, F. V. Pires took a position at a small technical college in New England. The pleasure of mentoring young colleagues and a wealth of personal experience in the engineering trenches are the inspiration for *Cygne Rouge*, along with the author's penchant for world travel and love of dance. F. V. Pires is a pseudonym.